Fermata

Cellars

By Gwen Alyce Clayton

Rivervine Publishing LLC
Ashland, Kentucky USA

First published in the United States of America by Rivervine Publishing LLC.

ISBN: 978-0-578-67037-9

Cover photography by Kristine Logan. Location: Country Heritage Winery, LaOtto, Indiana.

Fonts used: Interior—Garamond, Copperplate Gothic Bold. Cover—Bookman Old Style, Rage Italic

Dedicated to Eddie, my hero.

Prologue

THE PASSERBY

I didn't wanna get involved. All I wanted was a break from the heat; a bit of shade and a patch of grass on this sultry summer day were all I was hoping for.

My car had run out of gas a ways down the road, and the filling station was still quite a walk from my current location. The sidewalks were so damn hot, and the only shade within walking distance was this massive oak that was just standing there in the middle of a traffic island. The heat was getting to me and so I decided to stop and rest a bit before filling my gas can.

When I was a kid, Rivervine had lots of shade trees, cool soil and soft grass. Walking from one part of town to the other in the middle of June wasn't as miserable as it is today. Now there's just pavement—nice, hot pavement. The heat rises in waves like ghosts escaping their oppressive pall of asphalt. The oak was the only speck of nature I could see. It must have had my soul on speed dial because it called to me, insisting that I take quick break to grab some quality time with Mother Nature before putting the gas in my car and heading home to catch the game on TV. I answered in humble servitude, but had no intention whatsoever of finding God or having any kind of prophetic revelation.

I must tell you, I don't go for any of that funky New Age stuff—talking to trees and all that meditation crap, but something weird happened while I was under that oak, and I swear I'm not making it up. I sensed a voice, but it wasn't like a sound my ears could hear. It was as if the tree was talking to my mind–ESP or whatever you call it. It kept telling me to go to the old hippie winery and ask for Doina. Who the hell Doina is, I don't even know. Never heard of her. It freaked me out big time, almost to the point where I was just about ready to check myself into the loony bin. Sadly, my insurance doesn't cover mental illness, so I blew off the game and decided to go wine tasting. I mean, what the hell—how often do *trees* talk to you? Besides, if I were going insane, I might as well tie one on before they wrap the straight jacket around me.

I filled the can, fed the tank, and headed to Fermata Cellars a few miles away.

The long gravel driveway was packed with cars that were *leaving*. No one fought me for a place to park right up front near the tasting room. As I got out of my car, I stared at the giant stainless steel vats poking their heads over the rustic roof of the winery itself. A few feet to the right was the tasting room. I pushed the door open and walked inside. Taking a look around, I saw the shelves were bare; they were normally filled with t-shirts and kitchen stuff. A short, stocky, dark-haired woman with piercing blue eyes greeted me with a "Hello. Welcome to Fermata Cellars. I'm sorry, but we're closing. Were you expecting to do some wine tasting?"

"Yeah, I love your zin. Can I come back tomorrow?"

"I'm sorry but we just sold our last bottle. The city has pulled eminent domain and we have to vacate the property. We're completely out of stock."

"Well, damn! Eminent domain? What does that mean?"

"The government has the right to take our land and sell it. This place is going to be developed into a Spiritual Emporium."

I had no idea what a spiritual emporium was and really couldn't care less, so I just asked:

"Can I talk to Doina?"

"How do you know Doina?" the woman replied with quizzical suspicion.

"Oh," I struggled to think quickly for an excuse. "A friend

of mine just wanted me to say hello to her."

"Is your friend Romanian?"

Oh, God, I don't know. What nationality is a fucking tree? It's from Oakdale or Oakmont or Oakland or wherever oaks are made.

"No, Californian."

"Interesting. Well, Doina is probably over by the farmworkers' quarters on the west side of the property. Most of the workers left several months ago, but some have stayed behind to help pack and clean."

"Okay, thanks. I'll just go and look for her."

"Good luck. She's ... hard to find."

"Thanks. Hey ... I'm real sorry about the city council and all that. I love your wine."

"Thanks. We do too, but we'll manage."

"Take care."

"Thanks, you too."

"Oh ... which way is west?"

"The sun always sets in the west, so follow the big yellow ball in the sky."

"Ah! Got it, thanks."

Noticing the contrived smile gracing her lips as we parted, I left and began heading toward the sunset, taking the chance to roam around the property one last time while enjoying the fresh air and cool outdoors. With twelve houses of worship already established in Rivervine, I had a hard time grasping the fact that everything around me was going to soon be bulldozed just so another church could be built. Fermata Cellars is the city's only winery. If I were Jesus, I'd rather eat my bread and fish in the middle of this beautiful vineyard instead of sitting on a slab of concrete that's completely disconnected from my father's perfect creation.

Just as I was starting to get frustrated with the future of this town, fiddle music started to play. It was a soothing sound for the most part, except for a high-pitched string that kept going out of tune, annoying the bejeezus out of me. Heading in that direction to check it out, I could see something standing under an orange tree several yards from the tasting room—something that looked like an oddly dressed woman. Unable to see her all that well, I walked closer. Even as I got right up in the woman's grill, she was still almost transparent, like a hologram. She was wearing a ragged dress, bodice and apron that reminded me of one of those old-time paintings, or maybe a peasant woman at a Renn Fair. The sweat seeping out of her olive skin and soaking her long black locks grossed me out, as did her filthy bare feet and calloused hands. Yet, there was a type of beauty radiating from this woman; the glow in her big, brown eyes complementing her humble, sincere smile.

The fiddle, however, was not transparent. I was tempted to reach out and touch it, but I didn't want to interrupt her performance. The music sounded sad though, and a little bit angry.

The woman held the instrument over her right shoulder, just the opposite of what I have seen other fiddle players do. Not that that's significant or anything. I had just never seen anyone play violin left-handed before and I found it interesting.

Sitting at her feet was a thin, black piece of something metal. It also appeared to be real, and not transparent. While playing, she nudged it toward me with her left foot. After picking it up, I realized that it was a laptop computer. Curious, I opened the cover and pulled up the most recent document. The woman stopped playing and set down her instrument. Out of nowhere, a bottle of wine and a long-stemmed glass appeared in her hands.

Then she began to speak.

Mind you, I am not wealthy. I am not powerful. I am not the most intellectual person or the most persuasive speaker. But after hearing her story, I can no longer sit around and take justice for granted. I have to tell you what she said because her words freed me from the blissful bondage that kept me hostage in my self-centered, mediocre little world.

Her fragile hatred impacted me so deeply that I remembered every word verbatim, even though she spoke in extremely broken English complicated by a heavy Eastern European accent.

She was difficult to understand at first, but the more I listened to her spirit instead of her words, the more I got the gist. Here's what she told me ...

DOINA

So, you come hear my side of story? That is good. I need to get this off my chest. City council not listen. For one, I am not Rivervine citizen. For two, I am ghost. But I tell you my story. Maybe you listen.

My name is Doina. I am Comati—what you say, *peasant*, from Dacia. I live fourteen winters in my homeland. In Christian Year 1682, I meet rich lady from England. Doctors in her country tell her she cannot have baby. She come to Comati village, see if story true about our plants make her have baby. I am not doctor. I am girl who knows plants.

I work in my garden the day I meet her. I love plants. I love watch them grow—seed, sprout, giant bush. Many plants are magical. Everyone in my village knows this.

We are small village, only five families. No church. No marketplace. We trade with Romani friends if we not have something, but mostly, we make everything ourselves. Other village too far away for us go get something. Romanis bring what we need, and we heal their sick. We are all good friends. We all play music.

Romanis tell us story of terrible men who kill if people not kiss cross. But here in our tiny village so far from other people, we think we are safe. No one come way out here just to make us kiss some silly cross.

We are not Christian in our village, but we honor Magic Source. We see Source in dirt, water, air, plant, animal, sky— anything that is part of life. We see magic when plant grow from little, bitty seed. We see magic when woman bleed as moon move through sky; when lady not bleed, we know baby come.

When man is most happy, he makes magic juice. I want to make Radu happy like that. He makes my belly tickle when I look at him. I want to kiss him. Kiss tastes good with wine. Ah, I love wine. You like wine? Wine is good.

Rich lady like wine too. And she like my plants, especially the ones that make her have baby.

I tell her it is more than just plants. Moon must give blessing. Dirt must give blessing. Magic Source must give blessing. To get blessing, you must earn it. Moon does not care about jewels. Dirt does not care about money. Magic Source does not care about gold. Magic Source says life is like a spider web. Spider must be most careful. Each line makes all other strong or web fall apart. No two lines are the same. Each line is special. Each line is important.

Moon and sun understand. They dance with all other parts of life. We see moon and sun take turns for place in sky. Some days, sun shines more and days get hot—plants and animals busy. When moon shines more and days are cold—animals sleep, but fiddle stay busy.

Lots and lots of music in our village.

Long, long time ago, when I was a little girl, five Romanis need a place to sleep and eat. We welcome them, of course. One of them give me a fiddle. She say it is magic. Must only play when happy or music not sound right. At first, I think she is crazy. But after I play, I know what she mean.

The night I meet rich lady, I play fiddle after she drink special wine made from magic plants. After my family go sleep, I hear her and her man make lots of noise.

They stay with us a long time. Many nights, they drink wine and listen to me fiddle. Moon is big. After moon get small and grow big again, rich lady get sick. She tell me blood not come.

She is nice lady. I like her. I wish she stay. But her man have work in England. His company want him go New World, look for gold. Rich lady and her man want me to come with them. I did not want to go. I want stay with Radu. Rich lady and man say Radu can come with me to New World. Our parents say "no."

That night, men in black robes from north side of mountains come through my village. They carry big cross and tell us to kiss it. They say crazy story about we go to bad, bad place after we die if we not kiss cross or believe crazy stories they tell us with tips of swords at our throats.

Oh my goodness, I was so scared!

Men in black robes kill everyone in village, except rich lady, her man, Radu and me. Rich lady save us. She tell men in black robes spare our lives. She give them three pieces of gold. I live long time, but not in my village.

The four of us go to New World. Men in black robes stay in village and build church. I never see Dacia again.

We journey across ocean to town call Salem. Rich lady have her baby. I care for the boy.

In Christian Year 1692, people in Salem go crazy. They start call each other 'witch.' I do not know what 'witch' is, but people say I am one because I do not pray in their church. Doctors call me 'witch' because I heal people with magic plants. Doctors not make money. They want rich lady to buy medicine from them, not use magic plants. I am 'witch' they say.

They say Radu is witch because he watch the sky every night. He say sky know when crops are to be planted or when bad people will visit. He know it is time tell Salem goodbye.

Men in black robes want to tie rope around our necks and make us swing from tall, tall tree. Rich lady not let them. She tell me and Radu to run away in night. We do not know where to go but rich lady pack food for us and tell me I must take fiddle and teach my children to play; it is too magical to keep quiet. She kiss my cheek. I never see her again. I miss her. She is nice lady.

Radu and I run deep into dark, dark woods. Moon not shine that night. I know wolves and bears are hungry and think we are food. I tell Radu, "If I die, I want to be food for animal. I do not want to die because someone say I am witch."

I hear noise in bushes. For sure, I think I am food. But no. Man in black robe with cross around his neck stand in front of me. Three horses stand behind him. I never see him before. He look different from men in Salem. I think maybe he is ghost.

I start to cry—harder than I ever cry before. Radu hold me, try to make me stop crying. He cry too. Man in robe touch my shoulder and tell me he did not come kill me. He come to save me. When he touch me, I feel warm, not scared. He is nice man, not like other men in black robes.

He tell us get on horses—but not move yet. He say must wait until blue star shine.

I think he is crazy. Radu look at sky many, many nights and never see blue star. My mother never tell me of any blue star, and no Romani ever talk of blue star.

Man in robe say blue star is sign of magic door. When blue star sits on top of crooked sycamore, magic door is open. If we pass through magic door, we will be safe. So we sit on horses and wait.

Long time passes. Blue star finally show in the sky, but it is not over top of tree yet. Man in robe say we must wait until sycamore give blessing or magic door not open. The closer the blue star gets to top of tree, the hotter I get. I do not know why, but steam comes from the ground. Horses go crazy. Their feet move up and down and they make loud, loud noise.

Blue star gets very, very bright when it sits on top of sycamore tree. Man in black robe yell, 'Now!' and he snap horse's rein. We follow him. Our horses run very, very fast, faster than any horse I ever ride. Wind hit me so hard, and it is so cold, that I think my cheeks fall off my face! My hands hold reins so tight my arms shake.

Forest turns blue—beautiful shade of blue. We run all night long. Blue forest turn to blue meadow. But we not stop. Blue meadow turn to blue mountain. But we not stop. We pass more mountains and more meadows and more forests—all of them blue. We travel so fast that they are more like blue clouds with dreams of places we pass.

When the sun comes out, man in black robe tells us to stop. He say blue star closed magic door. We are on other side of the New World.

Everywhere we look, grapes vines wrap around trees. Man in robe say they are magic grapes. He want us care for them and make vine.

Then he leave. I do not know his name. I do not know why he saved us. But I like wine. I like the man in that black robe. He never make us kiss cross. I want to give him wine next time I see him, but his glass stay empty.

We share wine with people who call themselves Miwok. They are nice people. They live near river filled with big, beautiful fish. Miwok not care about gold in river. They care about deer and land and fish—and Radu and me.

Land is beautiful. Big, huge, blue birds fly across sky, and great big deer—bigger than Radu—roam everywhere.

Radu and I make noise many nights, but moon did not bless us with a baby until Christian Year 1695 when I survived my twenty-second winter. I want to teach baby ways of Comati village, like make wine and play fiddle. Life is good. My baby grow strong. When she grow, she become very, very beautiful.

She make noise at night vit Miwok boy. Moon bless them with baby. I smile when I see grandchild.

I die in Christian Year 1746. Since then, I am ghost. I see things change. I watch children of my grandchildren have babies, make whole new Comati village in New World. Some speak English and others speak Russian. Some have brown skin; the youngest have yellow. All my grandchildren are beautiful; especially Vondella, that is Comati word for *precious girl*. My greatest granddaughter, was born in Christian Year 1820. Man in black robe come back and make more wine. I am happy ghost ... until Christian Year 1841.

Rich man with white beard come to new Comati village from Old World, west of Dacia. He speak German and say he now own all the land by the river. He wants my Vondella to do his work. His men want her to dance. She always say 'no.' In Comati village, you do not make noise if you not earn love. Beauty is special, not wasted.

I do not like man in white beard. He does not care about Comatis or deer or blue birds or magic grapes. He only cares about gold. His men want pleasure but do not want to earn it.

In Christian Year 1848, my Vondella die for same gold that men in black robes take from rich lady in Christian Year 1687. Vondella is now ghost, like me. But she is strong ghost. She still plays magic fiddle and talks with people. I am ghost more than two hundred fifty years, but I am not strong enough to talk with people—until now. Anger makes me strong.

I am angry because I must say goodbye to deer and blue birds and magic grapes. I am angry because it is not true what people say about Comatis. I am angry because dragon will come soon.

Not long ago, Vondella make friends with a peddler here at the

new vinery. Before he leave, I see him put words on this black
thing here. He write the story of crazy people that make
Vondella and me leave. But Doina cannot read. Please, my new
friend, tell me the story. Let me pour you glass of vine while you
read.

Marketing Director Notes

by Manuel Chavez

PERSONAL AND CONFIDENTIAL

IEMMOL

Sunday, Feb. 2, 2003, 8:30 a.m.

I hate this fucking tie. My butt's all wet, and I'm sweating like a bracero in the middle of harvest season.

Before I could even get settled into the office, my bosses, Xavia and Sage Divinorum, handed me this wacky assignment.

"Go find a tree on the property and connect with it," insisted Xavia, the short, husky, blue-eyed, raven-haired matriarch of Fermata Cellars.

When I looked over to her tall, skinny, red-headed, freckle-faced husband, Sage, I had hoped he would contradict his wife. Instead he nodded in the direction of my laptop and told me, "Just type up whatever message the tree gives you."

Whatever ... message ... the tree ... gives you.

Oh dear, what have I gotten myself into? How badly do I need this paycheck? This is nuts.

And what's up with an Irish man like Sage having a Latin surname like Divinorum? Xavia swears she's also a hundred percent Irish, but her black hair, deep blue eyes, and short, stocky frame call into question any claim of her ancestors surviving the Viking invasions.

Whatever. Right now, all I care about is getting this stupid assignment over with. I feel totally dorky sitting here on the muddy ground wearing my good work slacks.

What a way to spend my first day as marketing director of Fermata Cellars. I don't know if I can handle this! Oh sure, I know my way around Fermata Cellars since I grew up here— working in the fields with my mother, picking grapes each season. I left to get my bachelor's degree in business administration, so I learned everything I'm supposed to about marketing. The three years I then spent pimping out overpriced wine at the Posh Portworks tasting room in Lodi (the most uppity winery this side of Napa) also gave me some pretty good wine-sales experience. But marketing director? That's a huge jump for a poor boy from Chiapas, Mexico. Oh my God, the responsibilities! What was I thinking?

Nonetheless, I complied and took on the task of finding a tree ... to talk to—one that had some sort of *message* for me.

Surveying the property, I asked myself, "How does one go about selecting a tree, and once it's found, how does one extract the respective message?"

As I turned my head west, the answer came to me. In the distance I spied the orange tree my mother and I planted outside the farmworker quarters back in 1980. I must have been about three-years-old. We had gone to a farmers' market one day and bought a big bunch of oranges.

"Mom, can I plant the seeds?"

"Let me ask Señora Divinorum."

Of course, Xavia said yes. Mom and I started the seeds indoors in little pots. If we had put them directly in the ground, they would have been dug up by one of the many feral cats that Xavia and Sage kept on the grounds to keep the rodents at bay. Most of the seedlings fell prey to my own neglect—I wasn't the most responsible caregiver at that age. Only one sprouted big enough to stick in the soil; we placed it a few yards from my bedroom window so we could watch it grow. Twenty-three years later, that tree has gotten pretty big.

I've never talked to the tree before. Sure, I've watered, respected and cherished them, but the whole tree-hugger act belonged to Xavia and Sage. So, here I sit going clickety-clack on the keyboard, wondering how the hell to strike up a conversation with a giant piece of wood.

The field workers better not catch me. If they knew I was doing something as weird as this, they would disown me altogether as a Mexican. Mind you, if I had a novena candle and a rosary that would be different. I could tell them I was saying a prayer for my mom or something; but me sitting here under a tree with a computer and a sloppily-knotted tie? That's heresy.

Fortunately, there are only a couple of workers this time of year and they're both in the vineyards pruning the vines on the North Slope, so I have the tree all to myself.

9:30 a.m.

After my last entry, I waited under the tree for a few minutes. A leaf floated on the breeze, kissing my cheek before it landed. I picked it up and started stroking it, developing a sudden fascination with the smoothness and elasticity of the fleshy green piece of nature. My imagination started to draw images of the veins being road maps of my life—a tour of my past, present and future.

I reflected on my childhood—the pain, triumphs and doubts: Like building playdough castles in Mrs. Rhoads' kitchen, or the burn of bile running up my gullet the first time a girl kissed me. The smell of grass as it went up my nose after I was knocked to the ground during a fight on the soccer field because someone had accused me of being friends with a witch. The time my throat clogged up with stage fright as my college graduating class received our diplomas while the band played "Pomp and Circumstance."

I assumed the veins were going to show me the roads not yet traveled. Until now, I had never imagined the future any further than this particular moment. My entire youth found me wanting out of the fields and into full-fledged American society. Today I'm there—having just turned twenty-six and reaching the highest goal of my life. I looked deeper into the leaf for an answer, but it wouldn't tell me the actual destination, only that I needn't fear the journey.

So now here I am, back in the office waiting for further instructions from Xavia and Sage. By some miracle my pants aren't stained. I keep checking my butt in the bathroom mirror, but I don't see any water or mud spots. Thank God.

Right now, my bosses are preparing for their gathering tonight.

The Divinorums and other business owners of Old Town Rivervine call themselves "Comatis." It's some foreign word for "witch" or "druid" or "weirdo"—I don't know. They get together four times a year for these giant bonfire parties. Growing up, being a Comati meant we were part of a close-knit community that took care of each other. I never needed a doctor or pharmacist, and I always had ample food and shelter, but everyone else thought we were freaks. As a Catholic, I kept my distance from the inner circle, even though outsiders labeled all of us as devil worshippers.

I don't worship the devil. I go to mass every Sunday at Saint Bernadette's. I take communion. I pray the rosary. I love the Comatis as part of my extended family, but they honestly do freak me out at times.

Xavia had mentioned something to me in passing this morning about tonight's ceremony being a celebration for some sort of ancient Celtic holiday called Iemmol, which apparently has something to do with the first stirrings of spring. I just hope they're not going to be sacrificing ground hogs or something.

Their rituals have always given me the creeps, not that I

ever actually went to any of them in years past. When I was younger, we could hear drumming and see flames burning as we watched from the farmworker quarters. The braceros were always invited to the parties, but we preferred to keep to ourselves. We realized the Divinorums were different, but never knew exactly what they believed in or what they did when they lit their big fires and started chanting. We all thought the Divinorums were Pagan, so we were afraid to go to anything that involved fire, strange noises and large crowds.

What made their rituals seem even creepier was that Fermata Cellars is supposedly haunted. We Catholics had always feared that the Comatis were practicing some kind of black magic that would somehow bring all the damned ghosts to life and turn Rivervine into a scene out of a B-grade horror movie. Despite the foreboding feeling lodged in the pit of my stomach, I have to admit that in all the seasons I've been here, nothing bad has ever happened. No little kids ever went missing. No disemboweled corpses have ever been found with satanic markings carved into their foreheads. No grapevines woven into crop circles. It's still creepy though. Whatever their religion is though, I know it's not Christian.

That's one thing that has always confused me, because Saint Bernadette's is the winery's biggest client. Fermata Cellars makes the church's communal wine. The Divinorums are even good friends with Father Armando. I guess the witch thing doesn't creep him out. Either that or he knows something the farmworkers don't.

Then again, the church is supposedly haunted too. I've never thought about it until now, but maybe there's a connection between Fermata Cellars' ghosts and the Crying Confessional. On Christmas Eve every year, there's a moaning sound that comes from one of the confessionals right after the Eucharist is celebrated during Midnight Mass. No one has ever been able to figure out the origin of the noise, and it never makes that sound any other time of year.

I always considered the church ghost to be different because Catholic sites are famous for their miraculous oddities. As for Fermata Cellars' specters, I don't think they really exist. They could probably be chalked up to weather phenomena or some other scientific explanation. They're a great tourist draw, though.

Having said that, tourism is a double-edged sword. Shopping in Old Town allows people to buy some really cool things and eat at the most awesome restaurants. These are places you won't find in Anytown, USA. Unfortunately, light retail, agriculture and hospitality jobs don't pay workers very much, and small-business owners struggle to keep up with the ebbs and flows of market demand. Meanwhile, chain stores and mini-mansions suit the needs of the yuppy class, who do make decent salaries in their respective fields. In addition to competition, small business owners, farmers and ranchers have to deal with the constant increases in labor and environmental regulations, which drive up costs. We just can't compete. That's why so many people in ag have started selling their land to developers like Edie Clark of EKC Development.

She's had her eye on Fermata Cellars for a long time, but the Divinorums won't sell. Lately, Edie's been hanging out at Fermanski's Coffee House. Not sure what she's up to there, but I'm sure she's plotting her next land grab.

The coffee shop owner, Mr. Fermanski, is also my landlord. Great guy, but ya know, as much I love coffee, I have to be honest ... I prefer Trails Saloon. Bobbie the bartender makes martinis just the way I like them—nice and dirty. If she ever dies, I hope she sticks around to haunt the place because I don't trust anyone else to make a decent cocktail. I just have to figure out what kind of tip to leave a ghost.

I'll bet Xavia and Sage would know. Of all the places in Rivervine, their *Black Land* has the most legends associated with it. The moniker stems from stories that the soil was pitch black for over a century before the Divinorums bought it.

According to legend, the area that is now Fermata Cellars, Rhoads' Home Herb Farm and Touchkoff's Bee Farm was black and lifeless from 1848 to 1969. A fire of unknown origin spread across one of Captain Sutter's lumber camps seven months after Jack Marshall discovered gold a few miles upstream. No one knows how the fire started or why the land stayed so morbidly fallow for 121 years, but once the Divinorums bought it, the trees and vines miraculously started to grow again.

One of the rumors floating around is that one of Captain Sutter's men set a Gypsy harlot on fire, and it's her ghost that continues to haunt folks throughout town. This Romani phantom supposedly took kindly to Xavia and Sage who were just a couple of flower children from San Francisco looking to get out of the city in order to live closer to nature and get away from talk about Vietnam (Sage was a soldier and Xavia worked as a nurse for the U.S. Army). The Divinorums will half-jokingly claim the Gypsy taught them how to care for the land, make wine and run a successful viti-business.

Other people say—all joking aside—that this same Gypsy ghost is evil. They believe she seduces lonely travelers and then brutally kills them. Well, I can tell you that no one in this town is lonelier than I am and I've never been seduced by any specter. However, sometimes when I'm really tired and my sense of reason wears thin, my imagination will wander and fear builds up inside me when roaming these grounds alone, especially at night. As soon as the sun starts to rise, the anxiety wears off and my sanity returns. It doesn't hurt to pray the rosary, though. It brings me a temporary sense of inner peace ... until the subject gets brought up again.

People can say all they want about this place being haunted, but as far as I'm concerned, it's all a bunch of bullshit. Xavia swears there are lots of ghosts, and that they only appear when they want to be noticed. I think she's been sniffing too much compost. Yeah, sure, strange things happen all the time—like music coming from the wine cellar late at night—but that's nothing unusual. Mexicans always have a violin, trumpet, guitar or something, and it wouldn't surprise me if, every now and then, they hid downstairs and sneaked a few bottles of vino while they played.

As for why the soil is so dark, the Miwoks frequently burned their land in order to control wildfires, prevent drought, and enable certain flora and fauna to proliferate. They might have had something to do with the Black Land, but the local tribe never claimed responsibility or declared this particular place as being particularly sacred.

Xavia is perfectly okay with the ecology of the soil remaining a secret, since she claims that the dark dirt is what makes her zinfandel grapes taste so magical, and says that if you solve the mystery, you'll spoil the enchantment. The high ash content of the soil works wonders for the fruit.

The other allegedly haunted place is the old Castillo manor across the street. It was originally owned by Dr. Ronaldo Castillo who croaked in the 1900s. I'm not sure who owned it before Scott and Leslie Tuft bought it in 1984—right before their daughter Erin was born. Scott and Leslie aren't part of the Comati crowd. They live full time in Redwood City and keep the Rivervine property as investment income, but when the Tufts are in town, Erin hangs out with Brigid Divinorum—Xavia and Sage's teenage daughter. Both girls are rather strange, but I think Erin might actually be a little disturbed. She's obsessed with snakes and is into that Goth look—black lipstick, nail polish, and hair dye. Her face must have half a dozen piercings and her ears look like she's got armor on the sides of her head. She also wears these trashy super-tight black vinyl skirts and bodices that are totally inappropriate for a girl her age, but I guess that's the style these days, so what can I say? One time, though, I saw part of her areola sticking out from her push-up bustier. I didn't say anything because I didn't want people thinking I was a perv for noticing.

Erin started hanging out with Brigid shortly after last Halloween. I wasn't here—I was still working in Lodi at the time—but I heard that Erin and four of her friends had been part of some crazy-ass cult that tried to sacrifice one of the Comati cats at their All Hallow's Eve ritual in the backyard of the Castillo estate. Something really bad happened, but Erin and her friends Tanya and Thomas escaped with the cat still intact. The other two boys made it to one kid's house, but they both died when their marijuana joint fell to the floor and set his bedroom on fire. Funny thing is, the coroner said the cause of both boys' death was shock, not burns or smoke inhalation, and they died before the fire even started.

Weird stuff like that happens all the time in Old Town Rivervine, which is why there are so many legends. Those stories spawned enough fears in people to keep buyers back in the day from purchasing the property, which is what allowed the

Divinorums to get a really cheap deal for it.

I'm glad they bought it because this place has given me a lot of happy memories over the years.

Mom and I came here every April and stayed until after the harvest, which was right around Halloween. When I was little, I hung out with the Rhoads family who own Rhoads' Home Herb Farm next door. Mrs. Rhoads homeschooled all of the workers' children when the kids were north of the border. When I graduated twelfth grade, Xavia helped me get a bunch of scholarships so I could go to college, and I worked here during my breaks all year round.

I haven't worked at Fermata Cellars since I left Davis. After graduating college, I took that sales job down at Posh Portworks, and it was there that I learned how things were done somewhere bigger and more successful than Fermata Cellars. It always bugged me that the Divinorums struggled so hard year after year. I just knew that there had to be a more effective way to sell wine, and I was hell-bent on learning how the outside world did things.

Mom stopped working the vineyards altogether three years ago when her brother back in Chiapas was diagnosed with Hepatitis C and she had to go home to care for him. She wants me to move down there with her, but fuck that!

Ah, Mexico, my homeland—I hate it! Sure, the climate is perfect for agriculture, but the good ol' boys that run things have fucked up the water supply, doused the land with chemicals and treated the workers like slaves. Americans—and their ever-precious passive consumerism—don't care who sacrificed what, so long as they can buy everything for under a buck without having to face the poor souls who suffered such inhumane conditions in order to bring a bunch of swill to the land of the free.

The Comatis follow different agricultural practices. The land and workers have always been treated fairly. Growing up, I never went without comfortable lodging, education or medical care, albeit somewhat non-traditional.

I'm honored to be back here once again.

I have to work weekends, but it's not like I have a social life anyway, so I'm not missing anything. I have Mondays and Wednesdays off. I find it weird that Xavia asked me to start work the day before my day off, but she wanted me to begin at the first of the pay period, which is Sunday (we get paid once a week).

Another weird thing about starting today is that tonight is not only Iemmol, but it's also Brigid's sweet-sixteen birthday party in the oak grove (which they call the *Oppidum*—another example of Comati jargon).

I want to give my bosses' not-so-little girl something special for such a milestone birthday, but I can't think of a damn thing. She said she didn't want store-bought gifts. Instead, she wants everyone to give her something homemade. I'm not very good with my hands. I can't draw. I can't paint. I have no artistic talent whatsoever.

I figure I'll go for an hour or two and hopefully slither home before the gift presentations take place.

My apartment is on the other side of the Vitis River, which makes my commute about a twenty-minute walk. My loft's on the second story and overlooks the courtyard where my landlord, Mr. Fermanski, has the most wonderfully scented roses. The garden is perfect for saying my rosary every morning.

Here at the office, my desk sits on a balcony overlooking the tasting room and gift shop so I can keep an eye on the bar traffic—and any shoplifters that might try to stash a t-shirt or souvenir corkscrew into their purses.

My best friend is Lily Rhoads—Mrs. Rhoads' daughter. We grew up together and were planning on attending college, starting in the fall of 1995. She got two years of higher education under her belt when her father died and she had to drop out of school to take care of the family.

Okay, enough religious and cultural discussion. Back to business, Xavia just popped her head in here to tell me she and Sage want to take me out to lunch for my first day of work. Before we leave, I should have something to show them I have not wasted the time they've trusted me with. I'm going to get to work on writing my submission to the Friday Business Wire for the newspaper.

Noon

I just wrote the first press release of my career, and I think it's brilliant considering the one-hundred-word limit the *Rivervine Tribune* gives submissions for the Business Wire:

Local winery introduces new marketing director

Fermata Cellars announces the addition of Marketing Director Manuel Chavez to the staff. Chavez is a native Rivervine resident who graduated from U.C. Davis in 2000 with a Bachelor of Science degree in Business Administration. His duties will focus on business development and public relations. Fermata Cellars, best known for its varieties of Zinfandel, Mead and Txakoli wine, is located at 9300 Vinifera Boulevard. Chavez may be reached at (209) 555-9300.

I intentionally left out any mention of the fact that I grew up here as a farmworker. I want people's first impression of me to be that of a professional, not a field worker.

We're off to lunch now. I think I heard Xavia and Sage say something about going to Fermanski's because it's near the

Tribune office. They make the best soups, salads and sandwiches. Coffee's not bad either.

3 p.m.

On our way to lunch, we stopped at the Tribune office where I delivered the hard-copy press release in person and brought the editor-in-chief, Glenda Fern, a bottle of wine (it's always good to suck up to the press).

"Ooh, thank you!" Glenda expressed, checking out the wine label.

"You're so welcome. Say, is David Lynne around?" I asked. David's the business editor.

"He's on vacation this week but I'm in charge of the Friday Business Wire for this edition," she answered, accepting my press release and a couple of business cards. "I'll make sure this gets in."

"Thanks so much for all your support."

She flashed a sincere but professional smile and shook my hand with a grip so strong, I thought she was going to pull my arm out of its socket. Who knew a woman could be so tough?

"Hey," she called out to me as we were leaving. "In the future, can you email press releases to us.? That way, we don't have to retype them. It saves us labor and you don't have to worry about typos."

"Yes, I know, but I wanted to meet everyone in person and this was a good excuse," I answered.

Glenda chuckled as I walked out.

When I got back to the grounds, my arm still ached so Mrs. Rhoads rubbed it with some of her eucalyptus ointment. I'm feeling better now, so until either Xavia or Sage give me another whacky assignment, I'm going to review the returned mail and update the customer mailing list—if I can find it on their computer somewhere. At some point in the near future, I need to start working on an actual marketing plan and developing a budget.

4:30 p.m.

That's all for today. I need to clean the bathrooms (all the tasting room staff members share janitorial duties at the end of the day) and finish getting ready for tonight's party.

I can hear the music already. People started showing up half an hour ago to light the bonfire, decorate the area and start playing their instruments.

The festivals are always held in the Oppidum. It's an area on the property where eight oak trees outline a circumference around a half-acre patch of bare land. The trees grew in this pattern the same time the vines started to regenerate back in the 1960s. Rumor has it, this is the spot where the original Miwoks' hun'ge (roundhouse) once stood.

Tonight, the area has been adorned with ribbons of silver, blue and gold streaming down from the boughs. The bonfire is lit in the center and an altar of some sort stands on the eastern border. The whole thing looks beautiful.

I'm dying of curiosity to see what goes on tonight. I'm a little nervous, but my gut instinct tells me I have nothing to worry about.

4:45 p.m.

The weirdest thing just happened. I was in the middle of scrubbing the toilet when I got an idea for a gift to give Brigid for her birthday. I threw off the cleaning gloves and ran back up to the office, typed up a poem in a nice font, printed it on good paper, and rolled it up like a scroll. I even found a piece of ribbon in the gift shop to tie around it!

I am not much of a poet, but I did manage to come up with this little ditty. It doesn't rhyme, but I think it's clever.

Blossoms

My dear Brigid

I have known you since you were a mere seed.

I have seen your parents nurture you,

Protect you from harm and promote your growth.

Today, you are here, a blossom;

sweet-smelling, beautiful and pure.

Soon, you will bear fruit

And it will be your turn to be the nurturer.

The nourishment you give will be sweet and substantial.

You will teach them to peel away their obstacles.

When the fruit is gone, they will seek comfort in your shade.

They will sit under you and find refuge from the heat.

They will ponder life as they know it, undisturbed—

Reflecting on questions

And you will give them answers.

Yet you will never lose the beauty and sweetness

that was found in your blossom.

May your seeds be bountiful.

Happy Sweet Sixteen, dear Brigid.

With love,

Manuel Chavez

February 2, 2003

Now I have to head to the bonfire area. I am so excited!

Monday, Feb. 3, 2003, 10 a.m.

Thank God I have Mondays off. The party was awesome, but my head is pounding today. I can't believe I drank that much, especially since it was my first day on the job and I was at a party given by my employer. But they kept filling my tankard, so I kept drinking. The fun I had was worth this hangover!

I would say close to fifty people showed up, and almost everyone had a musical instrument. There were fiddle players, guitarists, flutists, drummers and people playing things I had never seen or heard before.

By about 5:30 p.m., the ceremony started. We made a line in front of the Oppidum. Brigid stood at the front of the opening and waved each of us with this weird wad of burning sage as we walked in. It was apparently supposed to cleanse our auras. I don't know what an aura is, but I didn't *feel* any cleaner. Then again, maybe it was just because I was such a newbie that I didn't pick up on the details.

Once everyone had entered, we formed a circle and Xavia led us in a meditation. She had us close our eyes, take a deep breath in and then exhale. As we took a second breath, she instructed us to imagine ourselves as seeds in the earth; sitting there all winter long, storing energy, resting and dreaming about what we wanted to become. As we emerged from the ground, we were tender, young seedlings full of promise, yet easily damaged, so we entered into a ritual to help us gain the strength we needed to survive, flourish and play our respective roles in the cycle of life.

As we opened our eyes, the various shopkeepers took their places in this makeshift stage. After that, they did a few odd things that I couldn't quite follow—something to do with land, river, sky and a bunch of old Celtic deities I'd never heard of. I suppose I should have been weirded out, but they didn't do anything that was downright scary. Everyone kept their clothes on. The children were safe. No demons appeared out of the bonfire. It was just incense and candles and tossing stuff into the flames like pennies in a wishing well. I was actually kind of bored until it came time for the toasts.

We had each been asked to bring a tankard, chalice or goblet. When Xavia noticed I didn't have anything, she loaned me a large, wooden mug to use.

She went around the circle pouring a little mead in everyone's cup. Once everyone's cups were full, we were each asked to say something that we were proud of. Of course, I said I was proud to be back at Fermata Cellars and finally celebrating my first Comati gathering. I got a big round of applause for saying that.

Following the ritual, folks started presenting their gifts to the birthday girl—and polishing off the rest of the mead. Each guest took turns either performing a bardic piece or showing off the art they had created. When my turn came, I knelt on one knee, untied my scroll and read my little poem. Brigid cracked up so hard that tears started streaming down her face. I could tell she was touched by the sentiment, but couldn't help laughing at me for being so out of character. I'm normally not that big of a ham, but I had already had a couple tankards of mead in me and it was easy to get caught up in the revelry. I'm glad I was one of the first people to take a turn because the musicians and artists who came after me blew my little poem away.

My favorite performance of the evening was the fiddle/guitar duet between Lily and Brigid, although Lily's playing had an angry edge to it. She may be my best friend, but she doesn't talk much, not even to me. Her instrument has better communication skills than she does. I could tell that she's mad as hell about something, but she wouldn't tell me what happened. She always masks it with a smile and a vivacious melody. I would go so far as to call her a musical con artist. Most melancholy tunes are written in minor keys. Last night's duet was played in A major. If any other musician had played the same melody, the audience would have left feeling uplifted and good about life, but whatever torment Lily was experiencing was one that could not be hidden by major thirds. Her bow dug into those strings with an understated fury. I tried to tell myself it was just a song and I shouldn't take it so seriously, but her playing was so convincing that I couldn't separate the performance from reality. I was very close to believing she was going to lead us all in some sort of rebellion, and I was willing to march right behind her, no matter the cause. Her E string kept going flat, though. It's been an ongoing problem with that instrument as long as I've known her. She really should get it looked at—or just get a new violin all together.

Brigid, on the other hand, played like the virtuoso she's always been. That girl is so fluid in her fingering; she never misses a note. I don't know what Xavia and Sage are going to do once she flies the nest. They want to leave the winery to her when they retire, but her true love is music. Her heavy metal band—Brigid's Forge—is one of the most popular rock groups in the area. She has no desire to run Fermata Cellars. This is the only winery in Rivervine. It's been a tourist destination for ages, and unless someone else takes it over, Fermata Cellars won't have another generation in the family business and the town will lose a major cultural icon.

Maybe that's what tonight was all about—divination. What are they going to do in a future without the Divinorums? I pondered that questions all through the evening, even during the final part of the ritual when we all did this serpentine dance where we held hands and spiraled around the Oppidum. I was so drunk, I could barely stand up, but I stumbled through it anyway. Despite my inebriation, I was able to see Brigid at the tail of the serpent. She kept looking over her left shoulder and smiling as if ogling the person behind her. Yet, no one was there.

Now, I'm home and the room just filled with the scent of roses. That's odd for February. Mr. Fermanski's garden shouldn't be blooming for a few more months.

Tuesday, Feb. 4, 2003, 5 p.m.

I spent the day cleaning up the customer database, handling a few sales in the tasting room, and re-writing the wine descriptions. Here's what I came up with:

- **Pianissimo.** Our whitest Zin provides a soft taste with a hint of strawberries.
- **Tango.** Notes of plum and oak choreograph the sweet embrace between the Mission and Zinfandel grapes.
- **Requiem**. The bold, smooth flavors of rose hips and vanilla bring our deepest, darkest, old vine Zin to life.
- **Z Sharp.** This lively, piquant flavor of black cherry and nasturtiums comes from the feisty, young vines.
- **Saint Bernadette's White Rose.** This dry Txakoli variety hails from the Basque country, near the homeland of Saint Bernadette's Cathedral in Lourdes, France. Made from the *Hondarrabi zuri* grape, this special libation is available to the secular world as well as the sacred.
- **Jazz Mead.** Honey and spice and everything nice—that's what our mead is made of. This organic concoction of honey mixes with cinnamon, cardamom, nutmeg, cloves and galingale to make the flavor saucy.

Now I have to get ready for tonight's city council meeting. The Comatis and I are going en masse to comment on a new project that real estate developer Edie Clark has planned to go in right at the southwest corner of Vinifera Boulevard and St. Bernadette Lane. Clark wants to put in a chunk of mini-mansions along with a strip mall that includes a gas station, quickie mart, fast-food restaurant with a drive-through, and a bunch of other stores. The planning commission already approved the subdivision map last month dividing the land from one twenty-acre parcel zoned open space into ninety-five one-fifth-acre residential parcels and one one-acre commercial parcel.

It's now up to the city council to uphold the planning commission's approval, deny Clark's application all together, or approve it, but place additional conditions on it.

If this project goes in, it will drain the water table that we need for the grapevines, increase air pollution, fragment wildlife habitat, and detract from the charm that attracts visitors to Old Town Rivervine in general and Fermata Cellars in particular. Ideally, we would love to see the project denied, but that isn't likely going to happen. Realistically, we're hoping conditions will be placed on the project to protect the surrounding agricultural businesses. What those conditions might be, though, I don't know.

Wednesday, Feb. 5, 2003, 10 a.m.

It's my day off but I wanted to jot down my observances from the city council meeting last night. I taped the whole thing on my digital recorder, so I'm able to play back the conversations and give quotes where applicable.

When Clark's project came up on the agenda, Mayor Anza opened the public hearing, inviting Delbert Barton, the city's planning director, to give his report on the project.

"Clark's property sits right on the periphery of ag and commercial land," he disclosed. "Its present open space zoning was decided twenty years ago. The current planning commission has since approved the zone change to residential/commercial and the tentative map dividing the property."

Mayor Anza nodded and the stone-faced Barton returned to his seat in the audience. Project proponent Edie Clark then addressed the council, playing the economic boon card.

"Development equals income," she claimed. "The tax revenues this project will bring will help make Rivervine a vibrant community. This city must provide housing that attracts higher wage earners as well as stores and services that Middle America needs. If we don't, our economy will crumble. We have nothing else to offer them, but surrounding communities do. We have to be able to compete."

That all sounded well and good to the five city council members as they smiled and nodded in approval, but Lily called Edie's bluff. She was the first member of the public to protest the project.

"If this subdivision gets approved," she advised, "the landscape of Old Town Rivervine will be ruined and the quality of our air, water and soil will deteriorate. Barton's staff report claimed the water agency had enough water to serve this project without sacrificing the supply or quality of current customers, but those of us in the agricultural community are skeptical about such a promise, considering the tumultuous history we ag folks have had with developers. There have been way too many times when farmers and ranchers in other communities have been forced to reduce their water usage when residential subdivisions came in. Losing our water will destroy our livelihoods. I handed reports to the planning commission but they chose to ignore them. They can be found in tonight's agenda packet. I hope you all had time to review them. I have yet to read anything supporting Ms. Clark's position."

Cattle rancher Vern Bradley went next.

"All of us ranchers are worried that these new yuppie residents will complain about the smell and noise of the livestock and the traffic impediments our trailers and tractors will have on the roads. Right now, Rivervine has a nice, calm, quiet, peaceful lifestyle. We don't want that ruined. The planning commission didn't care about our concerns and approved the project anyway. Bet me dollars to donuts that if this project goes through, Clark will come after our property so she can further develop her empire. If she makes it too hard to preserve our way of life, we'll be forced to sell to her. She is a bully and will stop at nothing to get her way."

Vern's comments drew a huge round of applause from the crowd. The city council, however, was unmoved, except Mayor Anza, who smiled. She seems to be the only one of the five council members to genuinely support the agriculture industry. In the past, she has added conditions on development projects to help reduce the impact to ranchers and farmers. None of the others have given us any consideration at all. Tonight, three of the other four council members—Pam White, Perry Josephson and Brian Mann—rolled their eyes after Lily and Vern spoke. The other one—Warner McCain—remained poker-faced the whole time.

LeRoy Castro, who's the head of a group called Rivervine Citizens for Property Rights, was the next to stand up. He said it wasn't fair to dictate to a property owner what she can and cannot do with her land.

"Have either Rhoads or Bradley offered to buy the property from Clark?" he asked. "The American Dream has always been to have limited government intervention when it comes to private land use. Our Founding Fathers were stalwart advocates of the rights of people to freely acquire private property and use it any way they chose. Clark bought the property legally and she should be allowed to do what she wants with it. Anyone who doesn't like what she's doing should fork out the dough to stop her."

"That's a cop-out!" Lily interjected, rushing up to the podium. "Let big money ruin the community and push those without financial power to become subservient to those who own the gold. We don't live in a bubble, folks. What you do with your property impacts everyone else. As the saying goes, 'The right to swing your arms ends where my nose begins.' Besides, Clark has not specified any committed investors—no tenants for her strip mall and no buyers for her houses. She just wants the city council to take her word for it. Do you want Rivervine to fall to the fate of other California cities where too many developments are still sitting vacant, even years after their construction? The land is ruined. Toxins have percolated into the water table. Animal and plant species have been obliterated. The taxpayers are stuck with the environmental remediation bill while they suffer from cancer and other diseases from drinking poisoned water and breathing polluted air. You can't tell me that was written into the Constitution."

Unfortunately, Clark and Castro won the argument. At the end of the public hearing, White motioned to approve the project. Josephson seconded. Clark won by a vote of three to two—Mann voted with White and Josephson. Anza of course sided with us, but I'm not sure why Warner abstained. He didn't make any statements supporting or opposing it.

I don't know what to make of McCain. He kept awfully quiet all night, but I noticed his constant glare in our direction. It makes me wonder if he's holding out to snake the land to a more lucrative development project. Whatever the reason, I could tell by the look in his eyes that he has something up his sleeve. I don't have any proof, but I'm going to keep close tabs on him. Call it intuition.

Thursday, Feb. 6, 2003, 9 p.m.

This was an incredibly busy day. I spent the morning cleaning up the database and handling a few sales in the tasting room. As I was closing up this afternoon, Brigid's friends Thomas and Tanya came in.

"Hi Manuel!" they both shouted.

"Guess what—we're getting married," Tanya announced. "Is the winery available June twenty-ninth?"

They're both way too young to get married, especially at a winery— they're not even old enough to drink!

I feigned a smile and hugged them both.

"Congratulations!" I replied. "Let's go up to my office and I'll check the calendar."

We hiked upstairs and sure enough, June twenty-ninth was available.

"Lemme talk to Xavia to see if she can officiate. I'll get back to you."

"Great!"

I took down their contact information and promised to talk to my boss. In addition to running a business, Xavia is also a licensed minister. We have weddings here at Fermata Cellars all the time, and since she does run a religious group, she was able to get ordained, which comes in handy when arranging the exchange of nuptials.

At the end of the day, I accompanied Lily on her delivery rounds. She has a Community Supported Agriculture business and every week, she delivers boxes full of whatever she currently has in season to the various restaurants, residents and herbalists throughout the Riverine area.

"Ya always gotta make deliveries as the sun goes down," she told me. "This way, we can work the fields during the daylight hours, and then make some moolah at night. It's also cooler for the veggies. Plus, more people are available in the evenings so we can talk to them directly and get an idea of what they'd like to order in the future. It helps us plan next season's crops."

One of her usual stops is the local saloon called Trails. Bobbie, the head bartender, always takes several cases of Fermata Cellars wine while Chef Cheryl generally buys out Lily's remaining supply of fresh produce. With this still being the middle of winter, the only things in Lily's package tonight were spinach and rosemary.

The delivery van is a strange machine. The heater often goes out unexpectedly, chilling the entire vehicle, which is a good thing for the green stuff and the vino, but not so much for the human passengers who are then forced to endure the chilly and uncomfortable atmosphere. It's a strange chill too—the kind that shoots up your spine like a scene from a horror movie. It's not just the temperature that's uncomfortable. There's a dense nippiness that surrounds you and nearly suffocates you, as if there's someone sucking the molecules of oxygen out of the air. Maybe I'm just succumbing to this haunted winery thing. I'm sure it's probably just my overactive imagination, but the van really does feel like a tomb on wheels.

"The heater always fails along the trip to Trails," she assured me, as if reading my thoughts. "Then, it will mysteriously come back on during the ride home. Chalk it up to being a fluke."

Sure enough, by the time the van stopped in front of the saloon, the vehicle resumed the correct temperature and felt fine. But Lily, who never seemed bothered by the temperature fluctuation, looked in the back of the van and nodded her head as if gesturing to someone.

"Is someone coming with us?" I asked.

"What are you talking about?" she scowled, and then shot a glance back to the rosemary sprigs.

"Oh, nothing, I guess."

Maybe it was just my imagination.

We walked into the Trails business office where Lily introduced me to owner Desmond Taylor. I shook his hand and asked if he had any particular needs that I could help him with. He reiterated what I already knew about Bobbie the bartender being the one to order the wine, but as a friendly gesture, he walked me to the bar and ordered a couple of club sodas with limes so he could get to know me better. Lily and Cheryl started talking about lamb with rosemary, garlic and lemon.

"That would pair really well with a Z Sharp." I yelled across the room. "Just sayin'."

The two women chuckled and walked back to the kitchen. Bobbie, Desmond and I killed time by making idle chit-chat while Lily and Cheryl compared olive oils and discussed which one properly accentuated the spinach.

By the time Lily wrapped up her sale, I had convinced Bobbie to pre-order four cases of our 2000 Tango that was going to be released next month.

Lily and I headed to the van and once again, she shot an evil "be quiet" glance toward the back panel of the vehicle.

I do not understand that woman. She has always been strange, as long as I've known her. But now that we work so closely together, she's getting even more difficult to comprehend. How could someone I've known all my life seem like such a foreigner?

Friday, Feb. 7, 2003, 5 p.m.

I caught up on all my paperwork and called Thomas and Tanya to let them know that June twenty-ninth was a go and we could start making arrangements. The two love birds were thrilled that Brigid agreed to sing at their wedding and Xavia could officiate.

Then I got Bobbie's order squared away—placed her regular weekly order of one case of each variety, plus four cases of the 2000 Tango on the futures' list.

Friday, Feb. 14, 2003, 6 p.m.

Damn! I wish Valentine's Day were every day. We totally banked. This was our best sales event ever.

Valentine's Day always draws a crowd at the winery. Mrs. Rhoads and Xavia team up with the Touchkoffs who own the bee farm down the road to run a special every year: A Romance Package that includes a rose-scented candle from the Touchkoffs, lavender bubble bath and almond massage oil from Rhoads Home, a bottle of Tango from Fermata Cellars and two wine glasses with "Sustain My Love" etched on them with a giant fermata—the musical notation to prolong a note or rest. For the glasses, we use a heart as the dot below the arch. The package is a big sell at seventy-five dollars.

I checked the account records and the last three years, we sold an average of forty-five Romance Packages between February 1 and February 14 in years past. This year, we sold seventy. Our other wines and gift-shop items did killer too. Total profits were up sixty-three percent from last year. I'm not sure if it's some sign of the economy improving, or the fact that Valentine's Day fell on a Friday this year. A lot of couples came up today to make a four-day weekend out of it since Monday is Presidents Day. I'll bet there will be a ton of visitors coming in over the next three days too. My commission check is going to be sweet!

Wednesday, March 19, 2003, 5 p.m.
I was sick yesterday (just a little stomach ache) so I came in today to make up the time. This was definitely the strangest day yet since I've come back to Rivervine. In all my years of working in the fields, I have never experienced anything that genuinely scared me, or that I couldn't find a rational explanation for. Today, however, all kinds of weird things happened that I could not rationalize.

Of course, the whole town is abuzz with reports of President Bush announcing war against Iraq, but I would not have guessed our wine cellar would be affected. As soon as I got to work this morning, I heard terrifying noises coming from downstairs. My head filled with visions of vandals—unruly protesters looking to create havoc. It sounded like somebody was taking chains and whipping them against the cellar walls: *clank, clank, clank.*

Xavia rushed past me on her way downstairs with a bowl full of incense, insisting, "Don't worry, Manuel. I got it covered. Don't follow me."

What the hell is going on?

She was gone for four hours. During that time, the noises downstairs finally stopped, but upstairs in the tasting room, the lights kept flickering on and off, even though there was no storm that could have caused any electrical problems. The cash register repeatedly blinked, "Error #213" and refused to allow us to escape out of it or move on to the next data field. On top of that, I was trying to train our new employees, Christine and Holly, but that didn't go well.

"I always have to do the dishes," Holly whined.

Christine fired back with, "I'm a better schmoozer than you are, so let me work the bar while you keep the glasses clean."

"Ladies, please," I interjected. "Pour wine, and share the scrub work and the marketing. You're paid the same, so do the same. Christine, deflate your ego and run the dishwasher a time or two so Holly can build her schmoozing skills instead of being stuck doing the dishes all the time. We're Comatis. We bring our kin up to our level. We don't hoard the spoils while others do our grunt work. Housekeeping is in all our job descriptions so get to it. At the end of the day, I'll scrub the toilets while you two dust the items in the gift shop. And Holly, it wouldn't hurt you to smile and strike up a conversation with a customer, too. They're more likely to buy from a friend than a stranger."

They both grimaced at me, but I didn't care. I have bigger problems to deal with.

Oddly, Sage made a rare appearance in the tasting room for some unknown reason around two o'clock in the afternoon. He's usually in the winery itself working whatever magic he does with the blending, bottling and other tasks performed back there. He popped in just as Xavia returned from the cellar.

"What the hell happened?" I demanded as she emerged

from the cellar door.

She didn't answer, but instead shot me a forced smile and ran to Sage who embraced her so tightly, you'd think it was their last dance or something. They excused themselves to take a walk outside and were gone the rest of the afternoon.

The noises may have stopped, but the air in the tasting room still had that asphyxiating feel to it—the exact same sensation I get when riding in Lily's van.

Between two and three o'clock, nary a soul showed up at the tasting room, so we turned off all the lights in the building and put the Closed sign up. Christine and Holly went home at three thirty, but I stayed to make sure our bosses were okay.

About an hour ago, the Divinorums returned from their walk. Xavia grabbed an oil lamp, and carried it along with another bowl of incense back down to the cellar. Sage followed shortly afterward with his acoustic guitar. The scent of the incense wafted up to the tasting room and I could hear the faint sound of Sage's playing. I'm not used to hippie smells in a business setting, so I was a little put off at first. I don't think it's professional, but who am I to question the ways of the winery owners? Besides, we were closed, so it really didn't matter.

Their plan worked, though. Within a few minutes, things calmed down. The cash register started working properly, the lights stopped flickering and my spine finally eased up enough to allow my shoulders to peel away from my ears.

It's been very hard for me to concentrate on work today. The noises really freaked me out. That strange behavior from Sage and Xavia didn't do anything to console me either. When everything seemed to be okay once Xavia and Sage did their little incense and music thing, my mind wandered.

What were those noises and how did my bosses quiet them?

The Divinorums never explained what they were doing down in cellar, and I didn't dare ask. Their surreptitious behavior reminded me a lot of Lily when we make our runs to Trails— very distant and quiet, yet obviously scheming something they don't want to confess.

Thursday, April 3, 2003, 5 p.m.
Glenda Fern from the Rivervine Tribune stopped by the tasting room this afternoon.

"I'm not much of a wine drinker, but I had an urge to go wine tasting today," she announced.

"Well, I'm glad you came out. How are things at the paper?"

Glenda didn't answer right away. She just stared at me with a hypnotized countenance—looking past my eyes, piercing my skull with laser-like precision.

"The paper has its challenges, as does any business. Speaking of business how is the winery?"

Her voice was cold but diplomatic, as if I stood in the way of what she really cared about. Wanting to avoid any conflict, I continued our conversation while pouring a taste of the 2001 Pianissimo into her glass.

"Good," I answered. "We're expanding our business— renting out part of the tasting room for special events, revamping our website, and looking for distributors to sell our wines outside of Rivervine."

Glenda swirled her glass, raised it to the light, and then gave it a good sniff.

Not much of a wine drinker, eh? Novices don't do that.

"We'd be interested in doing more advertising in the paper," I added as she took a small sip. "Do you have any information on that?"

"I don't handle ad sales."

Glenda dumped the rest of the pour into the bucket.

"This is too fruity for my tastes. What do you have that's a little drier?"

I refilled her glass with some 1999 Requiem. She pulled a cell phone from her purse.

"Hello, Leonard? Can you stop by Fermata Cellars? I have a lead for you."

She hung up and swirled her glass once again before taking a small sip.

"Oh, now this is good."

She closed her eyes and took another swallow, letting the wine rest a bit on the tongue before trickling down her throat. With a sigh, she slowly lowered the glass and opened her eyes. Gazing at me once again, she paused a moment before uttering, "Wow."

She was so enamored with the Requiem that I hesitated to pour her the rest of the flight.

About fifteen minutes later, right as I finished pouring her a taste of Z Sharp, advertising manager Leonard Moore walked into the tasting room. Now that's what I call a motivated sales person—he can get here quicker than the pizza delivery guy.

He and I exchanged a taste of Txakoli for a folder stuffed with a rate sheet, ad sizes and color specs.

While Leonard and I were talking, Glenda meandered through our gift shop and sampled some mustard and picante sauce that we had out with crackers and bread. She finally interrupted us.

"I'll take a case of the Requiem."

That's a lot of wine for a newbie.

I grabbed a box and carried it out to her car. When I came

back, Leonard asked me what my advertising needs were.

"We're thinking of doing some cooperative advertising with other businesses, but we don't have any partners confirmed yet," I told him. "I need more information to present to them. This packet will do the trick. Thank you."

"When you're ready, call me. My card's in the packet."

He and Glenda left together.

Thursday, April 17, 2003, 11 p.m.

I am shaking as I write this. I would crouch down at the side of my bed and say a million Hail Marys, but I'm hoping that writing about this will get it out of my system and I won't be so fucking scared anymore.

Lily and I went on our regular errands tonight. While we were waiting for Bobbie and Cheryl to make themselves available (we had to wait a good ten minutes for both of them to get out of a staff meeting), we noticed Glenda Fern sitting at the bar. She had obviously been there quite a while—long enough to have a blank stare on her face and a meditative focus homed in on her cocktail glass.

Lily sat on the barstool at Glenda's right while I took the seat at the left and asked her, "How's the newspaper?"

"It sucks," Glenda retorted, never tearing her eyes off the ice cubes floating in her glass. "Ya know, I work my ass off sixty hours a week, hauling my cookies all over town, covering one story after another, interviewing the liars in city politics, writing, editing, designing layout and planning news assignments—all for a lousy twenty grand a year." She finally looked away from her glass and met eyes with me as she asked rhetorically, "And I'm supposed to *smile* when the publisher denies me a raise? In the meantime, my rent's been raised, my car broke down and my migraines are worse than ever. I can't afford this shit!"

She gulped her drink and slammed the glass on the bar.

Bobbie finally got out of the staff meeting and came back to the bar. It's gotten to the point where I didn't even have to formally order my drink; she just made my dirty martini and plopped it down in front of me. Lily ordered a club soda. I slapped ten bucks on the bar and told Bobbie to keep the change. She nodded in acceptance and smiled, then went to pour a pint of draft beer for the guy at the other end of the bar.

I continued my conversation with Glenda, asking her, "Are you thinking of a career move?"

"Oh, hell no!" she snapped, turning her stare from the glass to a location nestled deeply past my eyeballs. She lifted her chin snobbishly and boasted, "I am a journalist. That's just the way nature made me. I do what I do and I do it well." Her eyes returned to the melting ice cubes she was swirling in the glass. "I just need to supplement my income somehow." She burped and signaled for another whiskey and Coke.

"What do you mean by supplementing your income?" I asked, half expecting some sort of confession about developing a drug-dealing career or a prostitution ring.

"I am going to write a book about all the vampires in this town," she stated, grinning with an evil pride, "the real vampires. I am going to make Bram Stoker look like the Brothers Grimm."

She paused, furrowed her eyebrows, and leaned back in her barstool.

"Oh, wait. Have you ever read any of their stuff?" her speech becoming more slurred with each syllable. Then she looked at me, opened her eyes widely and said, "They actually were pretty grim. Maybe that wasn't the best analogy."

Gulping the last dregs of her cocktail, she gargled the liquid before letting it slide down her throat, and then started chewing the ice cubes.

"Maybe you should take it easy on the whiskey, Glenda," I told her.

"No!" she wailed at a decibel level loud enough for the whole bar to hear her. "Edgar Allan Poe, Ernest Hemingway, Mary Shelley—all the great writers made friends with the bottle. Besides, sheeee likes whiskey and I want to connect with herrr better, so *I* am drinking whiskey.

"She also told me if I wrote her life story that I would make a MIL-yun bucks. Then I could have a real house and, and, and a car that didn't break down every month and, and, and I might even be able to buy myself a city councilmember or two."

Then Glenda made some noise that sounded like a cross between a burp and a hiccup.

"Who is 'she'?" I asked.

"The main vaaammmPIRE! She's, she's, she's (pointing her index finger at me with each round of 'she's') the one who lives in your wine cellar (hiccup). Surely you've seen her. She's a BEE-U-T'Ful, dark-haired, left-handed violin player."

Glenda gestured as if playing violin.

"She's elegant and bold, just like Count Dracula," the editor continued, "But she didn't have fangs or blood dripping down her face."

"How do you know she was a vampire?" Lily disputed. "Did she try to attack you? Did she tell you she was a vampire?"

"No," Glenda slurred. "She did not uuuuh-tack me. She (heavy sigh) said that she wanted me to write her biography so the world would know how real vampires live and die."

"Real vampires?" Lily condescended. "What's a real vampire?"

Glenda paused, struggling to remember the details.

"Well ... she hasn't told me exactly yet. Ya know, I've only met with her once, and one's life story cannot be told in just one session. I plan on meeting with her lots of times during the course of this project."

"And what's in it for her?" Lily patronized.

"I don't know ... the truth I guess," Glenda replied, still slurring but starting to sober up a little with each attempt to remember the alleged conversation. "Maybe her soul will be set free or something. We didn't really go into detail."

"Did she tell you her name?" Lily baited.

"Yeah, but I don't remember now. I think it was Merlot or Chardonnay or something winery-sounding."

Then she yelled out, "Hey Bobbie! One more!"

As the bartender made a fresh drink, I noticed she put very little whiskey in the glass and a whole lot of cola. When Bobbie handed Glenda the drink, I just chuckled.

Lily fell suspiciously quiet. I wasn't sure if her silence was a means of refraining from embarrassing Glenda any further or if she actually knew something about these vampires and wanted to keep their dark, sinister secret.

Okay. So I admit I'm scared. This ghost business has been difficult enough over the last twenty-six years. Working at a supposed haunted winery is one thing (by the way, Xavia claims it isn't haunted ... it's enchanted). That's easy to believe given the past of this former gold-panning town with its rich history of gambling, drinking, prostitution and dirty deals. But that's just ghosts—unsettled souls of the dead who need to find their way toward heaven. But I draw the line at vampires! They are *not* real. What's next? Frankenstein's monster? Zombies? Ghouls and goblins?

I returned to my conversation with Glenda, changing the subject in hopes of settling this uneasy feeling in my stomach. "So ... what did you think of Tuesday night's city council meeting?"

"Bullshit as usual," she snickered, swirling her drink, continuing her gaze into the miniature sacred well of ice and alcohol that rested between her hands. "That new subdivision in The Heights—it's all about Edie Clark."

The Heights is another one of Clark's mini-mansion projects; this one's on the other side of Rivervine from the one that got approved last February. The Heights is already under construction.

Looking deeper into her glass, swirling her whiskey and Coke faster with each rotation, Glenda started rambling like a cynical shaman.

"You realize what she's doing, don't you? Back in the 1980s when the city was writing its general plan, a bunch of parcels got designated as 'commercial' because the soil and water had too much arsenic and other mining-related pollutants for it to be classified as 'residential' or 'agricultural.' A 'commercial' parcel didn't mean anything back then because we didn't have these big box stores that used a lot of water and generated tons of effluent. People bought those parcels because they liked the scenery—never thought about doin' anything with 'em. Now Clark is gobbling up those parcels and actually doin' sumpin' with 'em. Once she gets her grubby little hands on the property, she's having the city planning department rezone them as 'planned development' so she can chop 'em up into strip malls and cookie-cutter houses. Nobody cares about the pollutants in the water table. They just want cheap houses and a minimart on every corner ... I hope all those yuppies die of cancer!"

From across the room, Cheryl finally signaled for Lily to come into the office. They only stayed a few minutes as all Lily had tonight were mushrooms, thyme and nasturtiums (the flowers are edible; Cheryl chops up the mushrooms and mixes them with cream cheese and thyme, then stuffs the flowers and bakes them). I stayed with Glenda while they were talking. When Cheryl and Lily were done, I shook Glenda's hand goodbye, telling her I'd buy her lunch sometime soon. Once again, she nearly pulled my arm out its socket. I have to remember to just wave goodbye to the editor next time I see her.

I still had to take care of Bobbie's order, so I told Lily to meet me in the van. When I finished my business and headed toward the vehicle, I heard Lily say to someone, "Where do you get off telling people you're a vampire? You're not a fucking vampire!"

As I walked closer, Lily quickly fell silent.

I opened the passenger door, fearing for my life as I stepped into the van of doom.

Oh my God, there's a vampire in here.

I kept an eye open for bats and wolves, and hunched my shoulders around my neck so nothing could get at it. This was worse than being at a seventh-grade summer camp when everyone's telling urban legends they swear are true.

Lily kept awful quiet and had a look on her face that reminded me of my mother when I was younger. If I acted up in public, Mom would wait until we got home so she could scold me in private. In the meantime, she would walk around with that stern wait-until-we-get-home countenance. I asked Lily, "Are you mad at me or something?"

She shook herself out of the gaze and said, "Hunh-uh! Why would you think that?"

"You're not talking much tonight, that's all. So what do you think of this vampire stuff Glenda was talking about?"

She rolled her eyes and matter-of-factly stated, "Manuel ... you've been here just as long as I have. If there were vampires at Fermata Cellars, you and I would have seen them. All of us would be walking around with bites on our necks. People would either drop dead or metamorphose into blood-sucking zombies. Besides, with all the garlic we have planted on the property, do you really think any vampires would be hanging around? I think Glenda had a bad dream last night. Between that and the alcohol, she got an idea to write a novel. That's all. Trust me; there are no vampires in the Divinorums' wine cellar."

So what were those noises last month?

My sense of logic tried to tell me I was being silly, but something inside my psyche inspired me to go to bed with my Saint Christopher's medallion around my neck. As I started to feel myself fall asleep, I gazed at the full moon shining through the bedroom window and wondered if some werewolf was going to pop out of my closet or from under my bed. I jumped up and headed back to the laptop.

So here I sit at almost midnight, believing that if I faced my fears and wrote them down, they would go away. I've done that now so I'm going to go back to bed and try to fall asleep without having nightmares of lunatics munching on spiders and flies. I also want to know what exactly is going on in that wine cellar and what it has to do with the war in Iraq.

Friday, April 18, 2003, 8 a.m.

I woke up feeling totally refreshed. No nightmares as I had expected. Last night, after I wrote my last entry and went to bed, I lay my head on my pillow and found myself starting to erratically chant, "Hail Mary, full of grace ... " Mr. Fermanski's flowers in the courtyard must be starting to bloom because the scent of his roses filled my room more prominently than ever, even from my second-story apartment with the windows all shut—very tightly. The rose scent was beautiful and wonderful—very comforting. I even thought I'd felt my mother brush her hand against my forehead and kiss my cheek. I drifted off to a very peaceful sleep. No vampires. Whew!

Friday, April 25, 2003, 5 p.m.

I've been spending my mornings lately taking a cup of tea and sitting under the orange tree. I still haven't gotten any inspirations from the tree itself, but it's just a nice way to start the day—fresh air, happy memories and the taste of peppermint sliding down my throat. It just puts me in a good mood. I even made friends with a little racer snake. I used to be afraid of snakes, but this little guy is actually cute and very sweet-natured. We've been hanging out together the past couple of weeks. He stays with me until I feel a leaf brush against my cheek. Then I head to the office and get to work. My new buddy just wiggles back up the tree.

Today found me finalizing my marketing plan. Didn't pour a single glass of wine or even scrub the toilet (Holly offered to cover my janitorial duties since she saw I was so busy; that was nice of her). I submitted my plan to Xavia and Sage and they said they'd get back to me by the end of next week to give me the go-ahead or not. I figure I will need a budget of about $12,000. The website will cost about $230 to have professionally redone. I'd like to get some promotional items, like wine glasses filled with candy that I can drop off during prospecting calls. Those should run me close to $284. A tri-fold brochure (two thousand count) will cost $500, and a newsletter printed four times a year and mailed to two thousand people will cost $4,880. If I can bump up our advertising to six times a year in *Organic Wine Today*, have a weekly display ad in the *Rivervine Tribune* plus its website, and get a listing in the *Annual California Wine Guide*, our advertising costs will be about $1,280. I'd like to invite the other businesses to join in a cooperative advertising campaign where we share the costs and promote the whole Old Town business district. I'd also like to have a big festival—like a street fair—and hold it at the end of harvest season. I figure I'll need about $2,000 in seed money for that.

Tuesday, April 29, 2003, 5 p.m.

Got the thumbs up from Xavia and Sage on the marketing budget. Throughout the week I have been contacting business owners in Old Town Rivervine. All twelve businesses are willing to invest in cooperative advertising: Fermata Cellars, Rhoads Home Herb Farm, Enchanted Tule Bookstore, Touchkoff's Bee Farm and Honey Factory, Rivervine Organic Nursery, The Muse Instrument Shoppe, Mai-wok Indian Trading Company, Folkways Antiques, Wicked Wings Clothing Company, Baast's Purr Veterinary Clinic, and Lovers Knot Wedding Wear.

Our next Comati ritual is a week from today. It'll be a good time for us all to flesh out details.

BELTANE

Tuesday, May 6, 2003, 10 p.m.

My fingers feel like rubber right now. I'm riding that same wave of euphoria I had at Iemmol, only this time I'm not drunk. Even though tomorrow is my day off and I could afford a hangover, I still restrained myself in terms of how much mead I drank. What I experienced tonight had nothing to do with alcohol. There was something in the air. I could feel it. This was the real shit.

My morning started off with the usual solitary tea ceremony under the orange tree. My racer snake buddy wiggled up next to me, looked me in the eye, then ran up the tree.

When I got back to the office, Xavia reminded me to bring a shiny object, such as a coin or piece of jewelry that I could part with for tonight's Beltane ritual. I didn't ask why. I just figured it was another one of their weird customs, so I played along. But at the end of the evening, I realized it wasn't the bullshit I expected it to be.

When I got to the Oppidum, I saw white, bright green and cherry red ribbons adorn the trees and glittery ornaments sparkle from the limbs. When it came time for the ritual, the Comatis had *two* bonfires this time. The smoke smelled different than the one in February. I couldn't quite place my finger on what they were burning—the scent of maple wood perhaps? The more I focused on the fragrance, I picked up oak, madrone, grapevine, manzanita, pine, alder, holly, and honeysuckle as well. I recognized each of these woods from the numerous brush piles we burned during the spring cleanup of the vineyard when I was growing up here.

Before entering the circle, Xavia led us in a meditation: "Welcome, everyone to our Beltane rite. Tonight, we celebrate the twain between the vernal equinox and summer solstice. This is a time of fertility, be it physical, mental, creative or financial. We appeal to the fae folk—our nature spirit friends—for assistance in showing us the paths to our desired blessings. Before we enter the Oppidum, let us take a moment to clearly imagine what we want to manifest in the upcoming months."

Everyone bowed their heads and closed their eyes for about a minute before she continued. I pulled out a golden Sacagawea dollar—the only sparkly thing I had—from my pocket and held it both hands.

"Now gaze at the shiny object and visualize the manifested goal reflected in the luster."

Another twinkling of contemplation befell the crowd.

"As you enter the circle tonight, you will walk between two fires: One is purification and the other is fertility. Let the smoke from both of them smudge you. When the smoke clears, if your vision is to rid your path of something harmful that is hindering your greater good, toss your shiny object into the fire on the left. If your vision is to manifest a particular goal or reach a particular destination, toss your shiny object into the fire on the right. The fae will see your request and carry your plea to the Realm of Mystery. If the outcome benefits the greater good of the universe, the fae will guide you on a route toward manifestation. If something more appropriate to the greater good awaits you, they will deny your appeal and lead you on a more advantageous path. Have faith in yourself and trust in the ultimate beneficence."

As we entered the Oppidum, the percussionists rattled and everyone chanted:

"Welcome buds. Welcome fruit. Welcome fae in your

pursuit.

"Shiny trinkets, shiny souls; blessed be these shiny coals,

"Fertile field, fertile mind

"Fertile body, strong and kind."

When my turn came, I tossed my coin into the fire on the right and asked the fae to help make my work at Fermata Cellars a success. I nodded in gratitude and thanked these new microscopic friends.

Continuing to my place in the circle, I stared at the flames, letting them hypnotize me. The words of the chant registered in the back alleys of my psyche, but left the mundane level orphaned. Yes, I heard them, but they meant nothing to me as an ordinary person. Manuel Chavez no longer existed. This corporeal shell of a human being entered a realm where thought crossed through some unseen threshold to a new place filled with warmth and acceptance.

I am a Comati now. So this is what it's like—beautiful. Oh, the honor!

When it came time for the toasts, the mead made its way around the circle and we toasted to the nature spirits, sharing our hopes for Beltane.

I lifted my tankard and cried, "This Beltane, I ask for a fertile Old Town Rivervine. May we, as a community, grow in spirit, wisdom, and prosperity. And may I, as a newcomer, become part of this wonderful tribe and prove my worth to you all."

I felt kinda dorky saying that, but the words just sort of popped out of my mouth. A few people cheered and clapped. That made me feel good.

When the toasting finished, the balefire jumping began. Various couples—lovers, friends, family members—joined hands and, one couple at a time, actually leaped across the flames of one of the two bonfires.

This is the craziest thing I've ever seen. They're going to kill themselves.

But the flames weren't very high and amazingly no one got hurt. Lily grabbed my hand and I found myself bounding across a three-foot diameter of simmering coals of the western fire. We landed on the other side unscathed.

Whew!

During our potluck dinner after the ritual, Xavia gave me the okay to talk to everyone about my marketing plan. She normally has a "no business in the Oppidum" policy, but tonight, she made an exception.

"After all, it *is* related to the fertility of our business," she advised.

I went ahead and addressed the crowd:

"Hello, everyone. I have an idea to help promote our business district. It's a special event that will be called the Zinfandel Festival. We could hold it right at the end of harvest season in October or November. I'm picturing a street fair where we have a sidewalk sale, craft booths, children's activities, and baked goodies. We have enough overhangs on the buildings to shelter us if it rains, and the date will be right before the holiday season, which is a great time to attract shoppers before they spend their money elsewhere. If we all pitch in with a cooperative advertising campaign, we can get publicity at very little cost to each of us individually. In return, the event will bring customers to our area, raise awareness of our political struggles, and garner support for the preservation of our historical structures. I'm thinking we could have live music here at the winery and maybe even some games for the kids. We can easily rent pop-up tents in the event it rains."

Everyone seemed receptive. I didn't get any naysayers. The more we talked about the festival—from both a money-making and public-awareness point of view—the more we reached consensus of the need to collaborate. So many vacant buildings exist in Rivervine, and the shops that are open aren't making much of a profit. We need to do something to revive the area's economy.

We agreed to meet Thursday night at 6 p.m. at the winery to discuss organization of the festival.

As we kept talking, the feeling of euphoria expanded. Somehow, I was able to muster up the confidence to speak in front of these people. I didn't stutter. I spoke with clarity and conviction. I was leading a very important campaign. People were listening to me. They agreed with me. They respected me. I have never been in such an important position before. Mom would be so proud. I did this—with the fae's blessing!

Thursday, May 8, 2003, 8 p.m.

The merchants from the Historic Rivervine Mercantile Association met tonight to discuss the upcoming Zinfandel Festival.

"I think we should hold it Saturday, October 25 from 10 a.m. to 8 p.m." Xavia proposed. "It's the new moon closest to the end of harvest season. Plus, it's the weekend before Halloween, so we can capture the harvest fair crowd."

"That's not the only reason you chose that date, Xavia," Lily muttered.

"Yes, we owe her a great deal," our matron mumbled. "It is only appropriate that we honor her that day."

The other Comatis snickered. I had no idea who they were

talking about. Changing the subject, I asked, "What kind of children's activities can we do?"

"Face painting, crafts, I'm sure we can think of more," Candace Renborne chimed in. She and her husband Clive own the music store in Old Town. "We can do pennywhistle lessons or something. Let us think about it some more."

Clive nodded in agreement.

"Our beauty shop can do the face painting and hair braiding out on the sidewalk," Celeste Harmon from the hair salon recommended. "Another idea I think would be cool is to have a scavenger hunt where people look for things around town—either historical items or stuff from our stores,"

"That's a great idea!" I cheered. "That will really give people an appreciation for how unique Old Town Rivervine is."

"We can set up a stage outside the winery and bring in some live bands," Brigid suggested. "Brigid's Forge will play. In fact, I think all of us musicians should do a set. It'll be a real show of our local talent."

Her comment drew a huge round of applause.

When things settled down, Teresa Ceccerelli from the Sundried Tomato chimed in. "We have a portable pizza oven we can bring outside and cook on the sidewalk. We can sell pepperoni pizza for like ... two dollars a slice, and feature Ernesto's meats and Nadine's cheeses. We can also do a mushroom pizza featuring Al's famous fungi."

Everyone laughed. Al Espinoza grows mushrooms in Rivervine. His slogan is, "Al is one heck of a fun guy." Nadine Fremont owns the dairy farm, and Ernesto Gonzales is the local butcher. They're both big on raising their animals without hormones, antibiotics, or genetically modified feed.

"I think we have the start of something here," I

announced. "Let's be thinking about how much money we can all spend and come back with a budget. If we're going to hold it October 25, we need to get on it right away."

We all decided to regroup Friday, May 30. That should give each of us enough time to develop a budget and gather more ideas.

Friday, May 30, 2003, 10 p.m.

Our meeting with the merchants this evening was productive, but I'm too upset right now to type up my notes. I had carpooled with Lily so we could go back to her place afterward for biscuits and tea. Our appetites left us, though, as Sergeant Griffin from the Rivervine Police Department came into view. Startled at the sight of a cop on her doorstep, we got out of the car and Lily asked, "How can I help you, officer?"

No "Good evening, folks" or other pleasantry. He cut right to the chase.

"Edie Clark was found dead an hour ago at the Prospector Inn where she had booked a room for a two-hour period this evening," he noted, making eye contact with Lily. "The front desk clerk claimed she saw a woman matching your description meeting Clark in the lobby and accompanying her upstairs. The mystery lady was dressed to the nines in a slinky red dress, black high heels and diamond jewelry. When a neighboring guest complained of screams coming from the Clark's room, the manager went to investigate and found the body lying next to the toilet unclothed. No one saw the visitor leave the hotel. The cause of death is still under investigation by the coroner's office, but since you and Edie had a known adversarial relationship, I am obligated to investigate."

He handed Lily a search warrant.

"Lily has been with me since 6 p.m. and never left my sight during that time," I defended. "We were at a meeting with several other business owners who can vouch for our whereabouts. Lily was nowhere near the Prospector Inn at any time tonight."

Lily's reaction shocked me.

"I don't have any slinky red dresses, black high heels or diamond jewelry," she chuckled under her breath as she invited the officer inside. "They're just not my style. But feel free to look around anyway, officer."

I followed Lily while she guided Sergeant Griffin to her bedroom, showing him the contents of her closet and laundry pile. "See ... I'm more of a denim kinda girl."

Sergeant Griffin donned his Latex gloves and poked around with his flashlight.

"May I take a look at your garbage?"

"Have at it."

She led him to the trash can under her kitchen sink and then outside to the large garbage bin.

"Thank you, ma'am, that's all I need for now."

Lily walked him to his car and waved as the officer drove away. Then she came back to the house, closed the door and turned toward me with a confident grin on her face.

"Don't worry, Manuel," she consoled me. "Lots of people wanted Edie dead. Someone just dressed up like me to throw the scent off the real killer, but I have plenty of alibis. No one is going to frame me that easily."

"I wish I could be as convinced as you," I responded. "I'm shaking enough for the both of us."

Logic aside, the emotional reaction of having a cop waiting at your doorstep, accusing you of murder, even if you're guiltless like Lily is ... how can any human being have such cast-iron conviction? Innocent people go to prison all the time. What makes Lily think she won't be among them?

"Are you ready for tea and biscuits now?" she asked me, as if nothing had just transpired.

"No, thanks," I replied, too upset to eat anything, but not wanting to make a big deal. "I gotta go. It's late."

"Manuel, please don't worry about me. I'll be fine."

"Who do you think did it?"

"Don't know. Don't care. All I know is Rivervine's Enemy Number One is out of our way, and I have plenty of sources who can attest to the fact that I'm not the one who did the dirty work. This is a good night."

"It doesn't bother you that Edie was murdered? And that someone might have framed you?"

"Nope. Not at all."

I headed home, shaking my head in disbelief. I can't sleep tonight. Something very strange is going on and I'm really wondering what I've gotten myself into by coming back to Fermata Cellars.

Saturday, May 31, 2003, 12 noon

I'm still upset over Edie's murder. I have no appetite for lunch, so I might as well type up my notes from the Old Town Merchants' meeting last night—the notes I didn't get to last night because of Sergeant Griffin.

The merchants decided that if we all chipped in a hundred and fifty dollars, we can go pretty far with advertising and costs for things such as port-a-potties, decorations, supplies and renting a PA system for the stage.

We agreed that a fair admission price would be $10 for folks over 21, $5 for patrons ages 6 to 20, and no cost to children under 5. Price would include access to all games, entertainment and live music. Each guest over age twenty-one would be allowed to purchase an additional ticket for $5 that would include admittance to a wine-tasting clinic detailing the history of Fermata Cellars' wine, the proper way to taste wine, and how to pair wines with foods—featuring samples from the various Old Town Rivervine restaurants.

Net proceeds would benefit Baast's Purr's Good Samaritan program where strangers can bring sick or injured cats and dogs to receive free medical care. The animals would stay at the clinic until they could be adopted.

Wednesday, June 4, 2003, 5 p.m.

Lily just called.

"Sergeant Griffin told me the coroner declared Edie's cause of death was arachnid poisoning, and there was no sign of foul play," she told me. "A black widow's nest was found behind the toilet where Edie collapsed. Investigators believe the spider clung to her genitalia, and the unidentified companion must have left before the bite occurred. In fact, there were no fingerprints, hair or other physical samples to show another person was even in the room. Case closed."

"How can you be so calm?"

"Justice eases nerves better than chamomile tea."

"Not my nerves. I'm going to be sick."

Saturday, June 14, 2003, 12 midnight

Wow! Glenda Fern all dressed up and getting her groove on. The surprises just keep coming.

Lily and I walked to Trails tonight; we decided we needed the exercise and I just couldn't take another ride in the mobile tomb. Some good friends of ours from high school were playing in the band—a group called Hayden Opera.

Glenda was on the dance floor, rocking a low-cut black dress, high heels and—gasp—makeup. And boy, did she have some moves on her! I've never thought of her as the seductive type, but tonight, she sure could grind those hips.

Father Armando was with a group of Army personnel having some sort of military dinner. They were all dressed in their Class A uniforms and dancing to the band. Glenda had caught the attention of one of the soldiers and his eyes followed every twist of her chest.

Lily spent most of the night ignoring me and talking to Trails' entertainment director, Dalton Burnett. I think she's sweet on him, so I didn't mind. Goodness knows at least one of us needs to get some action. In the meantime, I enjoyed my martini and talked to the keyboard player, Joaquin Baptista, during the band's break. It was so good to reconnect with him.

"How've you been?" I bubbled. "Gosh, I haven't seen you since twelfth grade."

"I'm doing well," he answered. "I hear you're back at the winery, but you've moved up in the ranks."

"Yes, I'm the marketing director now. Do you have a day job or is the band your full-time gig?"

"I wish I could quit my day job. But no, I work Monday through Friday as the executive director for the Center for Mexican Freedom in Sacramento. This band is just my hobby. Music doesn't pay the rent. But at least the day job is rewarding, so I don't mind."

I couldn't stop staring at his gorgeous, soulful eyes; the depth of his character showed in the richness of his brown irises and the sunken depth of his eyeballs. My body tingled as we continued our conversation.

"Break is over," he announced. "Can we catch up after the show? It's only forty-five minutes longer."

"I would love to."

When the set ended, I noticed the soldier put his arm around Glenda and the two sauntered out together. Joaquin came to talk to me. A few minutes later, Lily interrupted us to let me know Dalton was going to be escorting her home.

My old friend and I ordered a couple more martinis and continued our conversation.

"Manuel, I need to be honest with you," he told me. "I'm gay. I have been all my life and I'm not going to pretend anymore. Homosexuality is an abomination in our religion, so if you want to disown me as a friend, I understand."

"No, please don't go. I want to talk some more."

The longer our conversation lasted, the more I realized how much I missed him. He is such a wonderful, caring, tender-hearted person and I was so grateful that we were able to re-establish our friendship.

After a while, he announced, "I have to go break down my gear. Can I call you tomorrow?"

"Absolutely," I answered, scribbling my phone number on a cocktail napkin.

I walked home alone and headed straight for the rose garden to say my hail Marys—didn't even bother running up to the apartment to get my rosary first. At one point, I begged Mother Mary to guide me through all this—Pagan bosses, vampires in the wine cellar and now a homosexual crush. I feel I have forsaken the Lord Jesus Christ, whom I love with all my heart. Why then do I have so many conflicting emotions?

Right at that moment, the scent of roses filled my nostrils

and a damp breeze blew against my cheek. The message in the wind reiterated what the orange leaf told me last February: I needn't fear the journey. That did more for me than Lily's chamomile tea. I'm off to bed for the night.

Sunday, June 15, 2003, 8 p.m.

My phone rang as I walked in the door getting home from work. It was Joaquin. We talked for nearly an hour, catching up on the lost years. He wants to meet for coffee sometime.

I'm so nervous. I can tell he likes me as more than a friend, and I feel the same way, but I've never had a romantic relationship at all, let alone one with another man. Plus, we're both Catholic. It just isn't permitted.

I'm so confused. My only option was to confide in Lily, so I called her as soon as I hung up with Joaquin.

"Can we have tea and biscuits now?"

"Sure, come on over!"

I knocked on her front door less twenty minutes later. The smell of fresh, hot biscuits made my stomach rumble. She already had the tea steeping.

"I think I might be gay," I confessed.

She chuckled.

"I could have told you that twenty years ago, Manuel. So what?"

"It's wrong!"

"Why? Oh, I forgot, you're Catholic. In Comati culture, it's no big thing. You're one of us now. Just accept who you are and bring Joaquin to our summer camping trip."

"How did you know it was him?"

"You weren't fooling anyone last night."

"I'm not ready to spend a weekend with anyone right now.

Speaking of last night, what's the scoop with you and Mr. Burnett?"

Lily shrugged her shoulders and huffed.

"Yeah, right, whatever. We hooked up. I gave him my number. If he calls, he calls. If not, I'm not wasting my time chasing after him."

"I hope you used a condom."

"Yeah, he had one in his wallet."

"That doesn't protect you from crabs or warts, though."

"Mom has ointment for those."

"Think he'll call?"

"Probably not. Why would anyone want me? I'm a poor farm girl with no bling, glamour, soft skin or sexy lingerie. I work hard three hundred and sixty-five days a year. Dalton can get a different bimbo every night, so why on Earth would he want me long term?"

"Because you're special and any dime-a-dozen glamour puss lacks your verve and character."

"Nice try, but I don't see him calling anytime soon. Having said that, a girl has her needs, so if he asks for nothing more than another booty call, I'm there. He is really cute."

"You are prettier than you give yourself credit for."

"Yeah, coming from a gay man, that's really comforting. Hey, maybe you should do my hair and makeup next time we go to Trails. Then I can woo him like Glenda rocked that soldier last night."

"Don't stereotype faggots, Lily. Not all of us have a sense of fashion and color coordination. I can't even knot a fucking tie."

"You haven't been part of the LGBT community long enough to earn the term 'faggot,' so watch your mouth, mister!"

"How does a straight chick get to pull rank on me?"

She just furrowed her eyebrows and pulled the biscuits out of the oven.

Monday, June 23, 2003, 7 p.m.

This weekend was so awesome! Too bad it ended on such a morbid note.

I went camping for the first time in my life. On Saturday, Xavia and Sage left the winery in the care of Christine and Holly while all the Comatis drove up to Lake Tahoe. We found a cute little spot way out in the middle of nowhere.

I struggled putting up my tent, but Brigid helped me get all the pegs tucked into the ground and poles put in the right places. Sage got the barbecue going and Xavia, of course, broke out the mead and wine. When evening came, we made a big campfire and cooked hobo stew (a mix of vegetables and meat wrapped in aluminum foil placed directly into the campfire). As usual, everyone brought their instruments and played music throughout the weekend. Clive Renborne from the music store even showed me how to play a few tunes on his pennywhistle.

I slept so well that night. The air smelled incredibly fresh; I loved inhaling the scent of pine trees as I drifted off to sleep. The sky looked incredibly dark and quiet. My whole spirit filled with happiness and a sense of peace. I wanted to feel this way every day. Even as we broke camp early Sunday afternoon, I rode that high of having such a close encounter with nature.

Unfortunately, that elation disappeared as soon as we pulled up to the Fermata Cellars parking lot Sunday afternoon. I was so glad Thomas and Tanya didn't carpool with us; they would have been heartbroken if they had seen what we came home to. Their wedding dreams would have been shattered for sure.

The entire vineyard seemed darker and gloomier than usual. The vines looked like they hadn't been watered in weeks. The stench of dead animals wafted in the air. The shrill of a crying woman echoed in the background. The whole thing was very creepy. We went into the Divinorums' house and noticed the ominous red light blinking on the answering machine.

Xavia hit the Play button. News we didn't want to hear came through: A real estate agent said someone was interested in buying the property. Such offers were hardly unusual, but this one had a completely different tone. I don't know who wanted the property, but something in this particular request made the Divinorums even more woeful than Edie Clark's various offers did. My bosses looked at each other, and then turned away as if focusing on the vineyard. Their gaze seemed stuck on the vines. Xavia whispered something to Sage.

"Do you want me to go too," Sage asked as his wife walked away, heading to the winery.

"No," she answered. "Stay here and tend to the vines. I'll be out to help in a little bit."

I wasn't sure if I should stay and try to revitalize the vines, or leave and give them some privacy. I ended up staying. The Divinorums, Rhoads, farmhands and I worked until nightfall watering, fertilizing and pruning the vines, picking up fallen leaves and doing everything we could to try to whip the vineyard back into shape.

But it was no use. The vines all looked horrible. It really made me lose my faith in the last two Comati rituals I'd been part of.

This is your magic, your witchcraft, Your Druidry? What a farce!

When I finished my work on the property, I went back to my apartment and prayed the rosary in Mr. Fermanski's garden.

The roses have been blooming for a few weeks now and they are ever so beautiful. I asked Jesus to forgive me for partaking in Pagan rituals and having homosexual tendencies, even though I didn't really feel guilty. I just thought that maybe the vineyard problem was God thinking I had betrayed Him or something.

Sunday, June 29, 2003, 11:30 p.m.

Miracles do happen after all! When I got to work this morning, the vineyard looked vibrant and beautiful. The leaves glossed in a healthy bright green and the tiny berries plumped up nice and firm for what's to be expected this early in the season. None of us can explain what happened, but we're awfully glad to have the vineyard back in shape in time for the wedding.

I was busy in the office throughout the day while the Divinorums prepared for the ceremony. Xavia insisted the wedding start at sundown—8:34 p.m. according to the almanac. When the tasting room closed at five, I headed straight to the Oppidum to help in whatever way I could.

As we were preparing for the ritual, our conversations centered on all the supernatural possibilities that could have brought the vineyard back to life.

"She didn't like the phone call, did she?" I overheard Lily ask Xavia.

"She was rather upset, yes."

"But she won't disappoint Thomas and Tanya."

"She has mixed feelings about this union but she loves her brother. She knows how miserable he is now, and wants to end his suffering."

That was the last straw! First, it was Glenda's vampires, then Lily's invisible friend in the van, the cellar incident, Lily's lookalike, the woman whose birthday is October 25, and now someone who wants to end her brother's suffering. This place *is* haunted and the specter is a ghost who wants to be memorialized as a vampire in a famous novel.

I had no idea what to do with this revelation. Do I say something or keep it to myself?

Then I started feeling dejected. Why hasn't this ghost appeared to me before? What have I done so bad that she feels she has to hide from me? Am I not Comati enough for her? Is it because I'm gay, Mexican, or Catholic? Good God, this vampire ghost is going to kill me because I'm a spick faggot, isn't she?

"Oh darling, stop," a woman's voice cried out.

Looking around, I saw no one.

"Stop what?" I asked. There was no answer.

Attempting to ignore it all, I took a deep breath and tried to distract myself by helping the other Comatis string the oaks together with silver and gold silk ribbons, leaving an opening between the first and thirteenth tree.

The altar looked quite interesting. A green cloth covered it and grapevines encircled a white candle sitting atop the Awen stone (a flat, circular piece of rock with three straight lines spread apart and topped with dots). The left side of the altar hosted a silver candle, golden chalice and pile of herbs with tiny white, pink and yellow flowers. The right side boasted a gold candle, small silver plate and a bundle of twigs wrapped with raffia.

The Renbornes brought some apple cider for the wedding chalice, and Brigid placed some homemade honey cake cut up in tiny pieces on the silver plate.

White linen covered the tables in the picnic area, and centerpieces made from grapevines, ribbons and gold candles sat in the middle.

Lily brought several baskets full of fresh flowers in a myriad of bright, beautiful colors. We tucked some into the centerpieces and scattered petals around the perimeter of the Oppidum. Xavia decorated the altar with some of the blossoms as well.

The Touchkoffs arrived with the food around four o'clock, but they still needed help setting up at the back of the picnic area. Some of the Comati kids pitched in and did what they could to set up tables and such.

The bride appeared wearing a billowy white sleeveless cotton dress with an eyelet ruffle, and a crown made of grapevines with flowers and ribbons tucked into the woven twigs. The groom donned a green cloak over his white tunic and black trousers that were tucked into his knee-high black leather boots. They both looked charming.

As the guests arrived, questions about the ceremony arose. Several people had never been to a Comati wedding before, and I could sense some of them were uncomfortable with the concept of a Pagan ritual. Unfortunately, I had never been to Comati wedding before either, so I was unable to answer their questions, but I was looking forward to witnessing one for the first time.

"It should be a beautiful service," I assured everyone.

I was already exhausted when Xavia announced that she was ready. I took a deep breath and helped her line up the guests the way we did for all the other Comati rituals. As each guest entered the grove, she waved the incense burner over them and asked them to make their way around the circle, walking clockwise until all of the guests were in. Sage played guitar and Brigid sang some traditional Gaelic wedding song. I couldn't understand any of the words, but it sure was lovely.

The bride and groom entered last, arm in arm, unlike

Christian weddings where the bride's father walks his daughter up the aisle. In Comati marriages, the couple starts their journey together as equal partners, not an exchange of property.

When the circle had closed, the various shop owners began their call to the spirits.

"Hail to the spirits of the land," Celeste from the beauty shop called. "I present to you Thomas and Tanya. May they be grounded in your strength."

"Hail to the spirits of the river," Teresa from the pizza parlor cried. "I present to you Thomas and Tanya. May they weather the emotional currents of life."

"Hail to the spirits of the sky," Ernesto the butcher shouted. "I present to you Thomas and Tanya. May your winds enable them to communicate gracefully."

At that point, Xavia returned to the center of the circle and lit the white candle. Tanya then took the silver candle and lit it from the flame of the white candle. Thomas did likewise with the gold candle. Xavia raised the silver plate of honey cake and said a little blessing in Gaelic before handing it to Tanya who fed a piece to her groom. Thomas then took the plate and fed a piece to his bride. After they both finished their bites, the couple went around the circle to each guest and offered them some of the cake; when the last guest had received a piece of honey cake, the bride and groom returned to the center of the circle and offered Xavia the last bite.

Xavia took her slice, then raised the chalice of apple cider and said another blessing in Gaelic. The couple once again offered each other a drink before going around the circle, offering each guest a sip of juice with the priestess taking the final mouthful.

After everyone had received their cakes and cider, Xavia

asked each of the guests to offer a blessing to the new couple. It was awkward for a lot of people. Not everyone was comfortable speaking in public. Some people recited toasts and poems that have been well known for ages. Others didn't know what to say, so they just passed. Those among the Comati crowd offered the most sentimental gestures.

"To Thomas and Tanya," Nadine from the dairy farm cheered. "May your love spark hope, health and the blessings of all that is whole and holy!"

The ceremony ended with the bride grabbing the bouquet of herbs off the altar and the groom taking the bunch of twigs. Xavia led the couple and all the guests out of the circle (walking counterclockwise) and toward the river, where the couple offered their bundles to the spirits as an offering of thanks.

From there, we did what we always seem to do at all Comati get-togethers—party.

Thursday, July 17, 2003, 11:30 p.m.

For some unknown reason, I couldn't sleep tonight, even after saying my rosary and having a cup of tea, so I walked down to Fermanski's Coffee House and treated myself to a caramel steamer while I plugged in my laptop to their Internet connection, intending to check my e-mail. Got there right before closing, but the kid who rang me up said I was welcome to stay and finish my drink while they started cleaning.

I sat down at the table with the Internet plug-in and logged on to my account. The whole time I was trying to type, out of the corner of my eye I thought I saw someone staring at me. Every time I turned to see who it was, the person was gone. It really got to be annoying after a while and I thought maybe I was just overtired or something.

That's when I heard a deep, gravely, nondescript voice yell, "That's my spot!" I turned to see who it was, but no one was there. I walked around and asked the kids cleaning up if any of them had said something to me. They all looked at each other and shook their heads as if I were crazy.

So I just packed up my stuff and headed out the door. The kids were all in the back cleaning the kitchen, but I still felt someone's eyes staring at me. I turned around one last time and a woman who looked like the spitting image of that bitch Edie Clark was sitting at my spot with a cup of coffee in front of her and a laptop computer. I could tell it was Edie, but her image, her coffee and her computer were all transparent; so much so, that I could see all the gift items for sale on the bookshelf behind her.

"Edie?" I called out.

"Yeah, it's me," she growled. "I have to tell you something, Mr. Chavez."

"Aren't you … dead?" I hesitated to ask, my mind in way too much shock to register her announcement that she had an explicit reason for talking to me.

"Yeah, I'm dead, okay?" she barked. "Doesn't mean I can't pretend to enjoy my day, now does it? This is my spot, my coffee and my computer. It's all I have these days, so I'd appreciate it if you would save this spot for me, okay?"

"Is that what you wanted to tell me—to save your spot?" I asked.

She took a sip from her coffee, then said in a much more calmed tone of voice, "No, no. I'm just new at this death shit and I haven't talked to any fleshies yet, so I'm a little nervous, okay? I'm sorry. Here, have a seat—before the kids come back. And keep it down. I don't want them to catch us."

She pointed to an empty chair in front of her. I slowly and cautiously did as she advised, taking my seat in front of her.

"I know you're all jazzed about your little mercantile group," she said. "But believe me; your troubles are far from over. Can you meet me here at midnight tomorrow? We need to talk when these stupid punks finally clear out of here, but I need a day to get my shit together before I give you the low down."

My nervousness at her request must have been pretty obvious because she rolled her eyes and threw her head back saying, "I won't hurt you. I promise. I just wanna talk. You have bigger enemies than me and I need to tell you about them."

The kids came out from the back and started putting the chairs on top of the tables. Edie disappeared.

I was about eighty percent scared out of my wits and twenty percent intrigued at what was happening. This was the first time in the twenty-six years I've spent in Rivervine that a ghost actually talked directly to me. I couldn't wait to hear what she had to say, yet this whole conversation caused my heart to race so fast that I thought it was going to thump right out of my chest. And who on earth was this enemy she mentioned? Was it someone I already knew—Warner McCain perhaps? Or was it a stranger coming to town? Maybe it was the ghost/vampire in the cellar.

I took a sip of my drink; it had already gotten cold. One of the kids started sweeping the floor. "Have a nice night, sir," he told me.

I headed home—nerves shaken and way too wired to sleep. I wish it weren't so late. I really want to call Xavia or Lily and ask for their advice, but then I thought, "What if Edie reached out to me instead of them for a reason? Could my own employer and best friend be putting me in danger? Maybe they can't be trusted.

Or maybe I'm going crazy."

In the meantime, I'm heading out to the rose garden to say my rosary again. I have no idea how I'm going to sleep tonight.

Saturday, July 19, 2003, 1:30 a.m.

I just got home from my meeting with Edie. I hesitated accepting Ms. Clark's offer, but curiosity got the best of me. I didn't tell anyone about the rendezvous we had planned. If Edie didn't show up tonight, I would know our conversation yesterday was just my imagination.

Fermanski's was locked when I arrived at midnight. I was surprised there was no alarm system, but since there had never been an incident before, I guess Mr. Fermanski never felt the need to install one.

I saw Edie's transparent image trapped inside, looking distraught and violently shaking at the glass doors as if trying to break them loose. But she couldn't quite grasp a hold of the handles; her hands just slipped right through. I tried jiggling the doors from the outside, hoping I could somehow make the doors give way. No luck. Exasperated, she gave up and leaned against one of the doors; that's when she slid through the glass to the outside and fell to the ground. We were both pretty shocked at that point, but at least the two of us were now on the same side of the coffee house walls. I tried to help her up but my hand passed through her arm.

I was nervous as all hell. Coming face to face with a real ghost was terrifying, especially the formidable Edie Clark. My stomach had all sorts of bile penned up and my brain had the hardest time concentrating. My mind kept thinking of excuses to leave, but couldn't settle on a good one. With my body being on auto-pilot, I ended up walking with Edie over to one of the tables on the patio and starting a conversation.

There must have been roses in the landscape somewhere because their scent permeated in the air.

"Sorry I'm such a klutz," she frowned. "I'm really having a hard time with whatever this new state of being is. I feel alive but my death certificate says Edie Clark, date of death: May 30, 2003. Cause of death: nerve poisoning due to *Latrodectus hesperus* venom. Can you believe that? I died from a goddamn black widow bite. I hate animals, all of them. I never had pets, not even a goldfish or a hamster when I was growing up. As an adult, animals got in the way of my business and I worked too hard to give a flying fuck about some dumb snail that was going extinct. Then I die from a black widow bite. Give me a break!

"Hey, I was not your typical silver spoon. I didn't inherit my business from a rich daddy; I founded this company myself.

"I launched my career right out of college. I started off as a real estate agent, got my degree from Stanford, then my real estate license, then my own office. My fortune skyrocketed the last few years of my life. People living in the San Francisco Bay Area couldn't afford the high cost of housing so they moved to Rivervine—a nice, quiet town with affordable housing, low crime rate and good schools. There was lots of land, mostly agricultural. Property was cheap. Folks didn't have to worry about the urban decay of the big cities, and it was close enough to San Francisco that people could commute to their high-salary Bay Area jobs while paying local-area housing prices. Sure, I could have devoted my efforts to fixing up the decayed parts of Sacramento instead of pouring concrete over perfectly good ag land, but urban infill was just too expensive. It was cheaper to rape Mother Nature.

"EKC Development became one of the foremost

companies in the four-county area. Its reputation centered on the ability to get construction projects done quickly, without forsaking building codes or overlooking quality issues. My business associates knew that when it came to integrity, my word was solid and my credit was good.

"Consumer groups heralded me as a champion for market-priced housing. I had a few upscale, executive-style subdivisions—but most of my work was targeted to young families looking to either buy their first homes or move up into something nicer. I took a lot of pride in seeing the smiles on their faces when they walked into their dream homes. My commercial properties brought in businesses that gave people jobs and put sales tax revenues in the city coffers.

"Federal, state and local officials loved me because my budget included a hundred thousand dollars per year in political contributions. Every city council member, county supervisor, local water agency director, assembly member, senator, congressman and even the governor were on my payroll.

"Yes, I was the anti-Christ but I always won the land-use battle. Rivervine was once prime agricultural land, but thanks to me, my money and my friends on the planning commission, much of it got rezoned. I could divide one-hundred-acre parcels into smaller lots and develop them for housing or business. Those poor farming bastards whose families had been here for generations didn't have the money to fight me. All they had to do was buy the land from me and they could do whatever they wanted. But they didn't have the money, so I won.

"Fighting me, by the way, was not an easy task. Not only did I grease the wallets of the powers that be, but I was also a pretty smooth talker. What do Americans love most? Liberty and self-reliance. Make them think those two things are threatened

and you have instant allies. All I had to do was convince
consumers that the tree huggers wanted to spit on their property
rights, take away construction jobs and reduce their property
values.

"So I get blamed for the poor air quality, overcrowded
schools, traffic congestion, stress on the water supply and the
demise of the ag industry. Oh, and I've killed a couple thousand
beasts in my life. Who gives a fuck? I invested three decades into
my company. Do you have any idea how hard it is to be a
successful woman in a man's world? The secret, I always said,
was to never make a man a pot of coffee, type his memos or let
him open a door for you. Otherwise, you'll never be anything
more than a secretary to him. I was a bitch and damn proud of
it—strong, independent, and smart. At age fifty-five, I had come
too far in my career to allow the Greenie Wienies to force me
into early retirement.

"I didn't make the rules but I realized my role in the game
and dammit, I played to win.

"The ironic thing is that the first large property I ever sold
was in 1969—right after I got my real estate license and long
before the housing-market boom. My first clients were a hippy
couple from San Francisco looking for a simpler ag-based
lifestyle. Yeah, that's right—I'm talking about your buddies the
Divinorums and the eighty-nine acres of unsellable property they
bought from me. The parcel was supposedly haunted—had been
abandoned for more than a hundred years. No one would
purchase it. When the Divinorums showed interest in buying it, I
thought they had dropped a little too much acid. But they paid
cash and put their names on the deed, so what did I care?

"Thirty-plus years later, I tried to buy it back from them. I
had a whole bunch of people interested in building a shopping

center in that area. The nearest mall is a good forty miles away in Citrus Heights. I figured if people were going to shop at gallerias anyway because those stores have the goods people want at the prices they wanted to pay, why make shoppers drive all the way into Sacramento when Rivervine could be getting their sales tax money? It wouldn't take much to convince the planning commission and city council that this project was more lucrative than your stupid winery.

"So here we are. Look at me know now. Did I go to Hell for this selfishness? No. I am here; in the spirit world or whatever this place is called, giving you my testimony. But guess what, baby, the Divinorums should have sold me their land because someone else has his eye on it and he ain't buildin' no shopping mall. He ain't gonna give 'em a fair price for the land and he's gonna do a helluva lot more damage than I would've."

"Are you talking about Warner McCain?"

"No. His buddy, Paul something-or-other."

I couldn't think of anyone named Paul who has been seen with Councilman McCain. But at least now I have a clue that something is up with the undertaker.

"So, what does he want to do with Fermata Cellars?" I asked.

"I'm not sure exactly. He's just been at my heels the past few months waiting for me to lose the deal. Like a snake in the grass, stealthy, but I can feel the malevolence brewing."

I sat silent for a moment, soaking in the revelation, not really sure how to process it. So I changed the subject.

"Hey, Edie, can I ask you something?"

"Sure, what?"

"Who was the woman in your room that night? Was it Lily?"

The rich bitch shot me a cynical smirk, rolled her eyes and started to chuckle, but before she could answer, she caught a glance of something behind me. The last words I heard from her were, "Holy shit!" before she disappeared.

A police car pulled into the parking lot. Sergeant Griffin stopped next to me and rolled down his window.

"Mind if I ask what you're doing here, Mr. Chavez?" he asked.

"Couldn't sleep, Sergeant Griffin," I answered very matter-of-factly. "So I just took a walk and this looked like a good place to sit for a moment and think; it has been a stressful few days, officer. I'm sure you can imagine. I just needed some time alone in the fresh air. I won't be long, promise."

His eyes canvassed the property. Seeing nothing had been vandalized or broken into, he nodded and asked, "Wanna ride home?"

"Sure. Thanks."

I hopped in the front seat. I had never been in a cop car before. There were far more gadgets and lethal weapons than a regular vehicle.

As he dropped me off in front of my apartment complex, he commented, "Boy, you can sure smell Mr. Fermanski's roses, eh?"

"Oh, yes you can; all year long, even when they're not blooming. Thanks for the ride, Sergeant Griffin."

"Anytime, Manuel."

I shut the car door and headed upstairs. My mission for the evening was done and I needed to get to bed. This is night two of staying up way past my bedtime on a work night. I don't get a day off until Monday, so I better get some shut-eye before I turn into a zombie and become the next menace to terrorize the city.

God, it's hard to sleep. I brewed myself a pot of Lily's anti-insomnia tea just now and am hoping it kicks in soon.

LUGHNASADH

Thursday, Aug.7, 2003, 8:00 a.m.

Sittin' under the orange tree right now—just me, the laptop and my little racer snake buddy. It's already hot this morning and my armpits are soaking my shirt. Above me hangs a bunch of young fruit dangling like Christmas ornaments and they're making me think of my career. I'm young and green, but hopefully over the next few years I'll grow into my skin a little better. I'm not quite completely confident in my skills as a marketing director, but my calling has definitely arrived. The Comati culture is growing on me too. The more I'm accepted into their inner circle, the more I realize how much they have to teach me and how much I've been missing these past twenty-six years. I am still uneasy with the whole Pagan thing, but they do have a sort of wisdom I respect.

Having said that, the vineyard incident from last June still looms over my memory. I was hell-bent on praying my rosary before work today just to show God I hadn't abandoned him. Mr. Fermanski's roses are in full bloom right now and gorgeous as ever. It was the perfect backdrop for saying my Hail Marys and Our Fathers.

It was a much-needed booster shot of Catholicism to guard me for the upcoming festivities. Today is the Comatis' big Lughnasadh shin-dig, marking the cross-quarter between the summer solstice and autumnal equinox. Lughnasadh is a bit different than the other holidays. We still have a private nightly ritual, but during the daytime, the Comati women run the shops while the men organize a few public sporting events—such as, archery, wine-barrel rolling and horseshoe tossing. We've blocked off a little clearing near the parking lot between the tasting room and vineyard where all the games will take place. I'm not good at sports so I'll be hiding out in the tasting room pouring wine. We're running a special on mead in honor of the Blessing of the Bees. Our slogan today is, "You buy one bottle and the hive buys the second." In other words, it's a buy-one-get-one-free deal.

Bees are a big part of Lughnasadh lore.

"We rely on our bee friends to pollinate the plants and trees that grow our food," Sage told me a long time ago. "At Lughnasadh, the flowers' nectar flow is at its highest, so the bees are at their busiest. We hold our sporting events to share our power energy with those who put meals on our tables."

Of all the Comati festivities from my youth, this is the only one I actually participated in—not the nightly ritual, just the sporting events. Archery was the one sport that interested me, but I haven't held a bow in ages.

Gotta get back to work There are some cases of mead in the cellar that I have to bring up, dust off, and put on display.

Friday, Aug.8, 2003, 8:00 a.m.

I threw my shoulder out at the archery tournament yesterday (Sage talked me into shooting during my lunch hour). Fortunately, I still have some of Mrs. Rhoads' eucalyptus ointment to rub on it, but it's hard for me to reach, so I'm hoping I can catch her sometime today so she can massage it into my muscles real good.

Physical pain is temporary, though. Memories last a lifetime. I will never forget Sage's advice:

"First of all, relax, for God's sake," he instructed.

I was stiff as a Christmas tree.

"Stand with your feet parallel to the target and shoulder length apart. Grip the bow handle with your left hand and level the front of the arrow above that little hole there," he said, pointing to a notch at the front.

"Now raise your bow level with the target, but keep your left elbow relaxed so you still have some clearance when you let go. Pull the string back and rest the cock-feather of the arrow on this nocking point right here (he pointed to a metal ring on the string). Raise your arm to shoulder height and hold the back of the arrow up against your index finger. Pull the string a few inches from the side of your face; the arrow should be level with your cheekbone. Focus on your target and shoot."

I released the arrow and away it flew.

"Now hold still. Slowly move your drawing hand back and keep focusing on the target."

I was way off—the arrow came nowhere near the target but at least it hit the board. Nonetheless, it was fun.

That night, the ritual was beautiful as always. The ribbons on the trees were a deep sage green and a shade of gold similar to the color of beeswax. The Touchkoffs had brought numerous candles that lit the parameter of the Oppidum. There was no incense this time. The natural scent of the beeswax was the only olfactory stimulation used.

The mead tasted especially good. Not sure why. It's the same batch we've had all year, but it seemed more refreshing and each sip made me feel more and more blissful—not drunk, just at peace. I felt at one with the bonfire, the people around me, the music playing, and the leaves of the oak trees blowing in the breeze. Xavia led a chant of some sort, but I couldn't focus on it. Some other voice ran through my head. It wasn't a speech my ears heard, but one that spoke to my psyche. Funny thing is that as the voice spoke, I imagined my racer snake buddy talking to me.

"You are a drone, Señor Chavez," the reptile announced.

"Your work is to bring fruit to your people."

The voice disappeared after that, but I knew my destiny had been confirmed: I must make Old Town Rivervine bear fruit once again. If this had happened a year ago, I would have been freaked out, but my gradual introduction to this occult stuff is making me think the Comatis are tuned in to a realm we Christians have forgotten.

I walked home in a state of reverie. As my head hit the pillow, sleep came suddenly and stayed peaceful all night. I woke up this morning feeling energized. During my walk to work, there was no indication of blight on the vines or any other ominous signs.

Noon

I love Lughnasadh! My review of the receipts of yesterday's mead purchases showed an increase of more and fifteen percent over the annual daily average, and an increase in overall sales up twenty percent. Looking at past records of mead sales throughout the year, I noticed the dates of the Lughnasadh festivities brought the highest volumes, and this year in particular was the highest. Only Valentine's Day had a higher average on overall sales. Blessed bees!

Wednesday, Aug. 27, 2003 10 p.m.

Xavia called a meeting with all of the Old Town merchants to discuss the Zinfandel Festival and its promotion.

"Tonight is the new moon," she wrote in an email to all the Comatis. "Since the Zinfandel Festival is a new venture, this is a perfect time to embark on new beginnings."

Although I personally believe she's just superstitious, the Comatis seem to think that the gravitational pull of the moon impacts the human brain somehow. Since she's my boss, I wasn't about to contradict her. Besides, I have no evidence to counter her claim.

The weather was warm enough to hold the meeting outside in the Oppidum. We brought in a few picnic tables and benches to sit on. The sun didn't set until about a quarter to eight so we had plenty of light.

We've all been talking informally about entertainment, publicity, scope of the festival and whatnot over the past few months. Tonight was a chance for all of us to put our heads together and get a plan in motion.

There was some debate as to whether or not we wanted this to be our Sauin ritual (the next Comati holiday which takes place around Halloween).

"On the one hand, the Zinfandel Festival is an awfully big event, and with Sauin being a week later, we could conserve energy by combining the two," Nadine Fremont from the dairy farm claimed.

"But the scope of this festival is different than the scope of Sauin," Lily countered. "Sauin has a more solemn tone and serves as an appeal to the ancient ones to help us survive the dark, barren half of the year. The Zinfandel Festival is a little too happy and secular in nature, plus it focuses solely on the contemporary shopping district instead of the ancestors."

"True, but Sauin is a celebration of the last harvest, and this is, after all, the last harvest of the grapes," Sage noted. "Plus, we're honoring the initial Comatis who were the ancestors who originally inhabited this land."

"It is of utmost importance to hold Sauin on November seventh," Xavia emphasized. "That is the midway point between the autumn equinox and winter solstice. October twenty-fifth is for the vines and the success of our local economy. Sauin is to show respect to all the ancestors."

After everyone debated the pros and cons of each option, we agreed to make the Zinfandel Festival a public event and keep the Sauin ritual private on a different date.

Wednesday, Sept.3, 2003, 11 p.m.

Joaquin joined me for dinner tonight. I slaved all day making beans—my mom's recipe—along with a fabulous Albondigas soup and a side of Spanish rice. I even made my own corn tortillas. When he knocked on the door, I greeted him with a big kiss and poured us a couple glasses of Tango while the soup simmered.

"So how's work?" he asked.

"Strange, it has been very strange. The rumors are true about it being haunted. But I can't quite grasp what all is going on."

I told him about the cellar incidents, Glenda Fern's weird behavior, and my conversation with Edie. I didn't expect him to believe me, so I kept things brief. Then I asked, "How have you been?"

"To be honest Manuel, I'm angry. The more work I do for the people of Mexico, the more I want to start another revolution."

He rolled his eyes and teased, "Maybe your ghosts can help me."

I stopped stirring the beans and froze for a moment as I remembered the voice from Lughnasadh address me as "Señor Chavez."

Changing the subject, I announced, "Soup's ready. Let's eat."

There was no more talk about ghosts, vampires or Mexico. We simply finished our dinner, cleaned the kitchen together and snuggled on the couch, watching some television show about ancient Mesopotamia. We both had to work tomorrow, so he didn't stay the night. I'm not ready for some things yet. Fortunately, he has never pressured me to go further than my comfort zone.

Friday, Sept. 26, 2003, 7:30 p.m.
I called Joaquin in a panic.
"I need to talk to you. Can you come over?"
"I'll be right there."
He arrived at my apartment shortly after five and found me in a state of complete terror. We sat on the couch and he wrapped his arms tightly around me.
"What the hell is wrong?" he demanded.
"I was in the upstairs balcony office working on some prospecting emails around noon today. Holly was on her lunch break and Xavia was filling in for Christine who had called in sick.
"Brigid's friend Erin Tuft walk in. The moment she took one step through the door, all of the electricity went out; even my laptop lost its battery power.
"Without saying hello or making eye contact with anyone, Erin headed straight for the cellar and let herself in. She was like, in a trance or something.
"There were about a dozen guests in the room who all stared at her for a moment, then set their glasses down and walked away—without buying anything. They were all mumbling amongst themselves as they left. Xavia didn't seem the least bit concerned.

"I ran down to ask Xavia if one of us should go after Erin. The teen may be part of the inner circle, but nonetheless, I've never seen anyone go down there unescorted, especially without any light to guide her way. I mean, this was a major safety hazard, wasn't it?"

Joaquin nodded and held me tighter.

"All Xavia could do was tell me not to worry about it," I continued. "So I go, 'Did you see her? She looked like a zombie. Don't you think that's a little strange?'

"And she responds with 'Manuel, she'll be all right.'

"So I asked her, 'How do you know? It just seems kinda risky to me to let a teenage girl descend a flight of stairs in the total dark, especially when she's acting like something out of a B-grade horror movie.'

"And then she told me, 'You're just going to have to trust me. Now, please, calm down. Erin will be all right—I promise.'

"How could I calm down? This was beyond just some hippie incense-burning and music thing like what happened last June. This time, a youth from the community was put in harm's way and I wasn't about to 'just trust' my boss."

"So what did you do?"

"The thought crossed my mind to fetch Sage who was out in the field with all the other laborers, but I figured he would have sided with Xavia anyway so it would have been a waste of my time.

"In a move of complete insubordination, I disregarded Xavia's orders and marched toward the cellar. The door wouldn't open.

"So I shouted out, 'Who locked this door?'

"And Xavia emphatically stated, 'The door doesn't want to be opened' as if I should have known better."

"Wow, that is creepy!" Joaquin interjected.

I continued my rant.

"I took a deep breath and analyzed the situation. I didn't hear any noise indicating that Erin had fallen down the stairs. There were no clanging sounds or screams of torture. No heavy breathing or moaning as if sexual acts were being performed."

"So, everything was all right?"

"Not exactly. Over the next hour, I tried to let it all go, but the electricity was still out. Through all this, I appeared to be the only one in a state of panic, which really made me question whether the Comatis were devil worshippers after all."

"Where does Satan come in?"

"When Holly came back from lunch, I told her what was going on and she didn't seem the least bit concerned about the oddities. I should have gone to get something to eat too—and escape my environs for a bit, but my stomach was in knots and I just didn't feel like leaving the scene of the crime."

"It doesn't seem to me like there was a crime," Joaquin reasoned. "These people are just different and you're going to have to get used to it. If not, you are going to lose your sanity. The electrical outage could have been a blown fuse or something. I still don't see what Satan has to do with any of this."

"Oh, it gets creepier," I challenged. "Not a single guest had come into the tasting room while this little episode was going on. This is our busy time of year; going this long without pouring for anyone is certainly not the norm."

"Well you didn't have any electricity," he noted, stroking my hair. "They probably thought you were closed. I'm sure the electrical thing was just a coincidence."

"How's this for a coincidence?" I asked. "As soon as Erin came back up the stairs into the tasting room, all the electricity

came back on and she goes, 'I just wanted to say goodbye'—
rather chipper for someone who was catatonic sixty minutes
ago—then she announces, 'I'm joining the Army.'

"Xavia ran around to the front of the bar and threw her
arms around the young woman and goes, 'If this is really what
you want, I support you. However, you do know my feelings on
military action in general, especially this war in Iraq.'

"Erin responded with, 'You know why I have to do this.'

"Xavia bowed her head and sighed a diminutive, 'Yes, I
understand.'

"I shook Erin's hand and managed to vocalize a 'good girl!'
pretending I was okay with everything that had just transpired. I
have no problem with her joining the Army, of course, but I
don't understand the relationship between her enlisting in the
military and today's electrical snafus, or why she would be acting
so stupefied when she walked in, yet completely jovial when she
walked out."

"So what did you do?"

"My eyes couldn't stop scanning her for nicks or bruises,
torn clothing or any other signs of damage. She seemed okay."

"So no harm, no foul, right?"

"I'm not sure. Xavia's a hard-core pacifist. I can't see her
giving any kind of blessing to just waltz into battle."

"This is really none of your business, so why do you care?"

"Because it's affecting my work. My laptop started
functioning just fine after Erin left, so I tried to finish my
prospecting emails but I couldn't focus. I kept stewing over how
I just lost an hour and a half of productivity over something so
freakin' bizarre."

"Take a deep breath," he advised, moving his hand to rub
my shoulder. "You're hyperventilating."

My breathing really was getting fast, so I inhaled and let out a big sigh.

"I started to get hungry since I hadn't eaten lunch yet, but I really wanted to see Father Armando and go to confession. However, the customer list lay in front of me and I noticed how many of them were from Saint Bernadette parishioners. On the one hand, I don't want the winery to lose any business; if the news somehow got out about this place actually being haunted, Fermata Cellars would be ruined. On the other hand, I don't want all these God-fearing Christians being duped into buying wine that's somehow tainted by an unholy force."

"What unholy force? Honestly, Manuel, I think you're making something out of nothing. "

"Am I really? What if the news I tell Father Armando upsets him so much he pulls his support for the winery and is forced to expose these vampires or whatever they are that live in the cellar? If I don't expose them, will there be a greater risk? What if there are no vampires to expose? I'll look like a total idiot and Fermata Cellars' reputation will be tarnished for nothing."

"Manuel, please, you're thinking too hard."

"Whatever … lunch was a communion wafer and a sip of Txakoli served by a waiter in a black clergy shirt. I now have the body and blood of Jesus Christ running through my veins, paired with some much-needed peace of mind."

"I realize confession is confidential—so you don't have to tell me what you and Father Armando talked about—but since you dragged me into this conversation, why are you still so upset after speaking with the padré?"

"He told me I was not the first person to express concerns about the church's relationship with the winery. However, no one has ever been harmed at Fermata Cellars. There are no bats flying around, wolves howling, or Boofa Ladies stealing children from the neighborhood. We have to take rumors at face value. For all we know, Erin may have been talking to Saint Michael in the wine cellar today. Maybe he was the one banging on the cellar walls last March. He is, after all, the archangel who leads the Army of God. If the two episodes in the wine cellar were related to the war in Iraq, there was a good possibility Saint Michael had something to do with them."

"That seems logical. As a Catholic myself, I would agree to that."

"Something, though, makes me doubt it's Saint Michael down in the cellar."

"What makes you so sure?"

"Why would a Catholic saint hide himself from me? Besides, Glenda talked about some female vampire with a wine name. But ya know what's worse?"

Joaquin shrugged his shoulders.

"I couldn't muster the courage to tell him about us. I didn't deserve that wafer."

My lover kissed the top of my head. It felt so good to be in his arms—safe and away from all the bizarre shit.

"I'm here now," he whispered. "Nothing can hurt you. This is going to be all right. We answer to directly to God, not the pope."

My love for that man in indescribable.

Tuesday, September 30, 2003 3 p.m.

A tall white-haired guy came into the tasting room today. Xavia and I were upstairs working on festival issues, but we heard the whole conversation.

"I'm Arnold Franklin, Rivervine Building Inspector," the man told Christine, handing her his business card. "We received a nuisance complaint yesterday about Fermata Cellars. May I speak with the owners?"

"Let me get the Divinorums," Christine responded.

Xavia ran downstairs while summoning Sage via walkie talkie. He was outside with the field workers harvesting grapes. Once the two owners were in the room, they invited Mr. Franklin upstairs to talk. I pretended to work on my computer so they wouldn't suspect me of eavesdropping.

"I understand strange events occur at the winery— unexplained noises, bizarre electrical outages that don't affect any other local customers, people mysteriously getting sick after drinking Fermata Cellars wine. Is that true?"

"I am unaware of anyone getting sick after drinking the wine, unless they have consumed too much," Sage answered, avoiding the topics of the noise and electricity.

"Mind if I inspect your electrical system? I also need to check your cellar for rats or other vermin that might cause noises. I'd also like to see the reports from the State regarding the winery's sanitation."

"Be our guest, Mr. Franklin," Xavia welcomed. "Manuel, can you print a copy of the reports Mr. Franklin is requesting?"

I did as instructed. The documents gave us a full clearance on sanitation issues.

Xavia and Sage led Mr. Franklin down to the cellar and around the premise so he could complete his inspection. After about an hour, the three came back to the tasting room.

"I see no obvious violations, but how do you explain the complaints? Is this place haunted? Do you have supernatural powers at work causing this nuisance?"

"We have no explanations, Mr. Franklin," Xavia scowled. "What laws are we breaking?"

"From a code enforcement stance, none that I know of, except there is a line in Title 19, Section 2.08 stating, 'Anything that is a nuisance—health, safety, noise, visual or otherwise—may be considered grounds for abatement.' That 'otherwise' technicality is why I'm here."

He rolled his eyes and scoffed, "If you do have ghosts, please apprise them of the law and ask them to back off. You are hereby given thirty days to rid your property of these nuisances. If the situation is not resolved at the end of the thirty-day period, the City may be forced to file official abatement charges, which will include recording a lien against the property owner and revoking your business license due to public safety concerns."

Mr. Franklin left without saying goodbye. Xavia and Sage marched down to the cellar. I hopped online and searched "Fermata Cellars nuisance." The first result showed a web group, headed by First Church of Rivervine's Reverend Paul Adamson, encouraging "any concerned citizens to file complaints against the winery so we can banish these demons once and for all." The site went on to show the history of the alleged hauntings and all the rumors of the *Black Land*.

So this is who Edie was talking about a few months ago.

When the Divinorums came back upstairs, I showed them my search results and they agreed that we need to email the rest of the Comatis.

Thursday, October 2, 2003 8 p.m.

The Old Town Merchants met this evening at the Trails Banquet Room. Xavia gave everyone the low down on the

Adamson movement and I told them about the online group.

"He's that wacko evangelical minister," Nadine from the dairy farm cried out. "The guy is nuts and corrupt as all hell."

"But he's rich," Clive from the music store interjected. "He has money and followers. Traffic near the church on Sundays is always bottlenecked."

"I have customers who ask me all about the lies he tells people about us—that we're devil-worshippers and stuff," Celeste from the beauty shop added. "I'm not surprised he's taking this course of action."

"Well, what are we going to do?" Sage asked. "His army is bigger and wealthier than ours. We need to be extremely strategic."

"We need more Christian allies," Ernesto answered. "Father Armando, our clients, family and friends—surely we can get some of them to testify on our behalf."

Xavia chimed in with, "From a public policy point of view, I don't think the City Council sees this as a religious war. The fact is, strange things do happen at Fermata Cellars and we have no defense. You can't really subpoena or incarcerate a ghost."

"No, but you can banish them, which is what Adamson wants to do," I advised. "We need to discredit him. What experience does he have in exorcism? If he has none, then how can he claim any ability to purge the alleged nuisance?"

"All he needs is an ally on the City Council and two sheepish council members to pull a majority vote," Xavia responded. "We know Mayor Anza is on our side. Pam White, Perry Josephson, and Brian Mann have been our main adversaries. God only knows where McCain sits."

"Y'all realize once Adamson gets control of Fermata Cellars, he's going to come after the rest of us Comatis," Al conjectured. "This is just the start of a huge war. By going after the biggest property first, he's setting a precedent that will make it easier to grab the rest of our properties later."

"I can go to the City Clerk's office tomorrow and ask to see the financial statements of council members' political campaigns," I offered. "I can see if Adamson is listed as a contributor, or if the council members have any vested interest in the church."

"Let's take a while to think about this some more," Xavia said. "And don't let it affect our Zinfandel Festival. We'll regroup after the new moon and talk some more. In the meantime, keep your ears and eyes open for anything we might need to know."

As the meeting wrapped up, Lily leaned over to Xavia whispered, "How is Zinfandel taking all this?"

"She's been awful quiet lately, but I'm sure she'll talk when she's ready."

Friday, October 3, 2003 noon

I went to the City Clerk's office to buy copies of the financial disclosure statements of all five City Council Members during the last two campaigns. Pam White, Perry Josephson and Brian Mann ran for election in 2002—Carmelita Anza and Warner McCain in 2000. Anza and McCain are up for re-election in 2004.

The documents showed that White, Josephson and Mann received heavy funding from EKC Development—Edie Clark's company. Anza was financed mostly from the local labor union and leaders in the environmental movement. McCain, however, had forty thousand dollars' worth of investors—each of whom contributed less than ninety-nine dollars. Candidates only need to disclose the names of contributors that donate more than one hundred dollars, so he obviously received more than four hundred and four private donations.

When I got back to the office, I searched that online group to see if any of the five council members were part of the discussion. None of their names showed up, but then, with online groups, it's easy to use ambiguous screen identities. As I scrolled through the posts, I didn't see anything that resembled anyone on the City Council; they all seemed to be posts from concerned members of the parish.

I did, however, notice there were four hundred and four members of the group. If each of them donated ninety-nine dollars to the McCain campaign, the math in his financial statement would add up.

At the end of my research, I had to wonder, "What motive does McCain have to ruin us?"

Between his odd behavior at Council meetings and vague financial statement, I'm still perplexed as to why he would want to shut us down.

Saturday October 25, 2003, 6:00 p.m.

The Zinfandel festival went very nicely, despite the Adamson bullshit. First thing this morning, he and some of his parishioners were out front demonstrating with signs condemning this event, but they seemed to have disappeared by ten o'clock. Don't know what scared them off. Maybe one of Glenda's vampires came out and bit them. Who knows?

Speaking of Glenda, she was one of the first people to show up at the tasting room today. Of all the people in Rivervine, she's the one person I did not want to speak to. But there was no avoiding her. Fortunately, she never brought up the nuisance complaints. I wonder if she even knows about them.

"Hello, Manuel," she greeted me with a grin. "Great weather for your festival, huh?"

"We got lucky," I returned the salutation. "I take it you got the press release I wrote."

"Yes, I did. Thank you. It was very informative. I do have one follow-up question, though," she said, pulling out her digital recorder. "What inspired you to put on this festival?"

"Other wine regions have festivals," I spoke into the recorder. "It was time we had our own. We're so unique here. We're the only winery in Rivervine, and we anchor the Old Town District. The other merchants all complement our business. A festival was just a great way to celebrate our little community."

"That's perfect. Thanks."

She clicked her recorder off and helped herself to a bite of the honey bread we had on the counter, and then headed downstairs. I didn't see her the rest of the day.

Dear Lord, please don't let her find any vampires ... or ghosts.

On my lunch hour, I walked around Old Town to check out the rest of the festival. The store owners had dressed up in Nineteenth-century garb, making the event that much more fun and festive. All the Comatis passed out candy to the kids and had a huge sidewalk sale, mostly emphasizing fall and Halloween items. The girls from the beauty salon were doing henna tattoos, face painting and Celtic braids in front of their shop. Frank and Tony from the vet clinic passed out literature on how to pet-proof your home for the holidays; their stuff even mentioned the importance of keeping black cats indoors on Halloween.

The entertainment was great. A few acoustic acts set up on the various street corners, collecting tips in their guitar cases. It was really charming.

The only amplified music was here at the winery on Sage's

makeshift stage. I wasn't able to watch most of the acts, but I could hear them from the bar. Fortunately, the Touchkoffs performed during my lunch hour so I was able to see their really cool Russian dance. Vitaly had a red shirt with a black vest, billowy pants and knee-high boots. Olga was decked out in a cute little red scarf and skirt with a white blouse and black vest. She twirled around and around while Vitaly did that bending and kicking thing you always see Russian dancers do. His knees are going to be sore tomorrow for sure.

Unfortunately, I missed the Mexican Dia de los Muertos dance. They came on right as I needed to get back to work. As much as I try to evade my own heritage, I have to admit that I enjoy certain cultural performances like that. Another thing I missed was the Miwok troupe. I saw them walk by with their flicker headbands and deerskin loin-cloths. I could hear their gourds and pipes from the tasting room, though, and couldn't help falling into a daze trying to imagine their performance. I snapped out of it as soon as the woman in front of me scowled for not pouring her next taste of wine. I couldn't remember if she had tried the Tango yet, so I gave it to her just in case. Her frown went away and I slipped back into my reverie.

The last act to take the stage was Brigid's Forge. They were definitely the loudest band. I didn't feel like I was missing anything being stuck in the tasting room during their performance. I heard every note perfectly.

We just finished cleaning up. Everyone is trying to be happy, but the melancholia is hidden behind an extremely thin veneer. There are so many mixed emotions with all that's been going on politically that it's going to be difficult to separate spirituality from the mundane world.

Tuesday, Oct. 28, 2003, Noon

Mr. Franklin delivered a harsh blow to Xavia and Sage this morning.

"We have received several complaints claiming the noise of the Zinfandel Festival exceeded the sixty decibel limit—a violation of the City's Noise Ordinance. All of these come after the deluge of complaints recently about the alleged hauntings. The City hereby begins official abatement procedures. You have fifteen days to request an Abatement Hearing with the City Council if you want to challenge the claim. Should you exercise—or should I say, exorcise—that option, a hearing will then be scheduled within the fifteen days after that. If you take no action within thirty days, the City will record a lien against the property and all costs of the abatement process will be at the expense of the property owners."

He handed them documents confirming the City's plans.

"How can you prove this place is haunted?" Xavia inquired. "And what codes are we violating other than the Noise Ordinance? We don't have live music events often. This was a one-time violation. You can't shut us down over that. We've been part of this community since 1969."

"You're right about the health and safety codes," he answered. "But it's still a nuisance. We've had more than fifty complaints about the unexplained sounds, electrical outages and whatnot. Fermata Cellars is a liability, even if all the wiring and other things comply with the Uniform Building Code. People don't feel safe here. It's the City's responsibility to provide for the general well-being of residents and guests who enter Rivervine's city limits."

The lights started to flicker and the temperature in the tasting room dropped about ten degrees. We all had goose bumps running up our arms.

"Is there a ghost in this room right now?" Mr. Franklin called out, heading for the door. As he walked out, he left with a final statement: "If so, you might want to leave this place if you expect the Divinorums to stay in business."

When the coast was clear, Sage mentioned to Xavia, "I think I need to have a little talk with our squatter," and walked down to the cellar.

I looked at Xavia and asked, "So what do we do now?"

"Request a hearing," she replied. "Let's have all of the complaints aired in a public forum and make the city look ridiculous for believing in superstitions."

I couldn't keep my feelings to myself any longer. I was scared shitless and my trembling diction made it evident.

"Speaking of superstitions, what, what, what's going on d-d-d-downstairs?" I fumbled, asking her point-blank. "Who's this 'squatter' that Sage is going to talk to?"

"She'll reveal herself to you when she's ready, Manuel. She's been watching you since you were a boy, and gave us her blessing to hire you earlier this year. Yes, she's a ghost—and a vampire as well. But it's not like in the movies. You're safe as long as you don't piss her off."

The stun of the news threw me aback, but I struggled to compose myself enough to quiver, "A v-v-vampire? So Glenda was right. She's writing this monster's life story. And Lily lied to me, saying it was all a figment of Glenda's imagination."

"Lily doesn't believe Zinfandel is a vampire. But I know it's true because I have personally fed her. Lily is also very protective of Zinfandel's secrets. You will learn them when the time is right. It's not for any of us incarnates to tell you."

"I take it this Zinfandel character is the Gypsy who taught

you to make wine?" I tried so hard not to squeal.

"Yes, she is the Lady of the Vineyard. We pay homage to her every chance we get."

"How can she be a ghost and a vampire? I thought they were two different things."

"She will explain when the time is right. Be patient, Manuel. I know this is all very upsetting for you to hear, but trust me; you have nothing to worry about. Take the rest of the day off. Go home and make yourself a pot of chamomile tea and find a book to read or something so you can get your mind off all this."

As I started to leave, the room resumed normal temperature. The lights stopped flickering as Sage came back upstairs and announced, "She's ready to fight."

"So shall it be," Xavia replied.

I think I'll stay the rest of the afternoon.

2 p.m.

Xavia and Sage just got back from filing a request for an abatement hearing with the City Council. I don't see how we can lose. Judging by all the codes I've read up on, we're not violating anything. Claiming the place is haunted can't be proven by any authority. Any reasonable government body surely wouldn't give credence to a collection of ghost stories ... even if they're true.

Tuesday, November 4, 2003, 10 p.m.

We had the abatement hearing tonight. I taped the whole thing on my digital recorder. Reverend Paul Adamson was there and able to sweet-talk the council into the most horrid thing I could ever imagine—it was worse than a scene straight out of The Crucible.

The evening started with Arnold Franklin giving his staff

report. All fifty complaints were read aloud. Then Mayor Anza opened the public hearing.

"Will the property owners please approach the podium?"

Xavia and Sage went to the front of the room.

"How do you respond to these charges?"

"They are absolutely ludicrous!" Sage contended. "We have been here for thirty-four years. Our winery has been the subject of ghost stories the whole time. No one has ever complained until now."

"Throughout the world, you will hear tales of ghosts haunting one place or another," Xavia added. "I admit we have had noises and electrical outages that may have been considered nuisances, but they have all been benign. No one has been injured. If this abatement goes through, it sets a precedent for other jurisdictions and we could lose many historical buildings throughout the state, the country or even the world. We strongly encourage the Council to dismiss the charges."

"Thank you Mr. and Mrs. Divinorum," Mayor Anza said. "The public hearing is now open. Would anyone like to address the council?"

That's when Adamson let it all out. Here's the transcript:

"Good evening everyone; my name is Reverend Paul Adamson and I am the minister at the First Church of Rivervine. I lead a congregation of more than four hundred evangelical Christians who are committed to returning America to its Christian heritage and exorcising the demons that ruin our blessed country. I am here tonight to address the nuisances coming from Fermata Cellars.

"My house of worship is named First Church of Rivervine for a reason. In 1941, the people of this city saw a need to establish Christianity in a town that had been plagued with sin.

Prostitution brought venereal disease to God-fearing folks who were unable to avoid the Devil's temptation. Many a good man died from opium overdoses, gambled away his day's wages, or found disease by women of ill repute.

"My grandfather, Otto Adamson built the First Church of Rivervine to offer Christian folk a healthier and safer alternative form of entertainment. The church held revivals, bingo games, and dances for young folks—free of any sexual pressure. Reverend Otto was known for his inspirational sermons that led wretched sinners away from their vices and helped them turn towards our lord and savior, Jesus Christ.

"Let me begin by clearing the smokescreens established by this group of heathens.

"Fermata Cellars is a doorway to Hell. In the nineteenth century, the Comatis—decedents from a lost tribe of vampires—used prostitution, tainted wine, and opium to lure innocent Christian pioneers away from God.

"When the god-fearing John Sutter found gold nearby, the devil offered him a deal: 'I'll give you all the gold in this here river if you and your men forsake your heavenly father and join me.' But Sutter refused, and that year, hundreds of his men burned in a horrible fire sparked by Satan himself. The land stayed as black as a funeral shroud until these two dope-smoking hippies from the unholy city of San Francisco came to Rivervine in 1969. They accepted Satan's deal. He made the land fruitful again—but this is not the fruit of God. The Divinorums claim to have resurrected the old Comati tribe and hold rituals throughout the year according to ancient customs with big bonfires and chanting and summoning the Pagan gods and goddesses. This is *not* the work of God.

"In 2003, the ghosts continue to haunt the premises,

wreaking havoc through electrical outages, loud noises and even unexplained murders such as the death of Edie Clark last May. Clark was a known adversary to Fermata Cellars and their Pagan allies. The Coroner declared her death was attributed to a spider bite, but witnesses claimed a woman matching the description of Comati Lily Rhoads was in the hotel room that night. These Pagans have the ability to shape-shift, leaving behind no evidence. Edie Clark died at the hands of these Satanists. Do you really want to allow them to continue their evil plans? If these Satanists are not defeated now, Rivervine will be overrun with the spiritual cancer they bring. The city's soul will be lost. Those vines are from Satan himself, as are all the plants and animals that mysteriously emerged from the Black Land. Fermata Cellars' wine is known for causing an extraordinary form of inebriation that is unlike anything produced by other vintners. Once people become drunk off the Devil's liquor, they are powerless against him. It is only natural that the Pagan Catholic Church serves this wine during its communion ritual.

"God has spoken to me and told me to offer the City of Rivervine a proposal. He wants to have these acres dedicated to our beloved Creator. It is the only way to rid the city of this Pagan pandemic. If you condemn this property and sell it to me, I will implement God's divine will.

"First, I will exorcise the demons of this land—send them straight back to hell! When members of my congregation stand on the perimeters of the land and begin our prayer vigil, we will be able to tell Satan to his ugly face that the good people of Rivervine rebuke him.

"Once the area has been spiritually cleansed, I will have every inch of Pagan influence torn down and covered with concrete—sealing the Devil's doorway to hell. Yes, this means demolishing historical and contemporary buildings and destroying the habitat of endangered species like the red legged tree frog, but the Almighty sees no value in preserving haunted houses and He certainly favors the needs of man over lower creatures.

"Then I will build a giant Spiritual Emporium over this doorway to make sure the Wicked One never comes back to disturb the good people of Rivervine. Sunday services will attract more than two thousand good Christians every week. Think of all the tax revenues housing, hotels, restaurants and other retail businesses will receive thanks to our presence.

"But that is not all I will do for the city. God has given me visions—great, wonderful visions. I see a school where children of preschool thru high school age can receive superior education in a Christian environment. We all know the failure of California's public school system and how violent our campuses are. We can build our own school where children are safe and educated properly. They will learn from day one, that Jesus is the reason our country is so glorious. He has given us Divine Providence and will not fail his chosen ones. Boys and girls will understand their role in society.

"Finally, the church will operate a Christian book store and a family gym. Ours will be the largest in Northern California. This will give us a literate, healthy society devoted to our lord and savior, Jesus Christ.

"As you can see, if you allow me to build my Spiritual Emporium, I will not only cleanse the land of the demons that will devour your souls and prey on your innocent children, but I will also attract parishioners who will spend residual tax dollars for the struggling City of Rivervine that will help pay for road maintenance, emergency services and other needs. God will take care of you if you take care of Him.

"Jesus and I thank you for your earnest consideration of our request."

As Reverend Adamson returned to his seat, the entire audience went into a bout of hysterics. I couldn't believe this was happening. This wasn't Salem, Massachusetts in the seventeen-hundreds. Weren't we beyond all this witch hunt bullshit?

The antics continued until Mayor Anza finally slammed the gavel down and called for order in the Council chambers.

"Reverend Adamson, I will not have you upsetting these chambers!" Anza cried.

She continued tapping the gavel until the chambers finally fell silent enough to hear her speak.

"Do you plan to pay taxes on your private school, bookstore and fitness center?" she asked.

"The First Amendment guarantees us the right to have our religious business carried on without interference from the government," Adamson replied. "We are therefore exempt from paying property and income tax. But the residual economic effects will be greater than any taxes you might earn from our humble church."

"Pay local taxes or keep your moral code out of our legislation," Mayor Anza dictated. "You can't have it both ways. Whatever 'God' you believe in can decide what is wrong or right, without government interference. If you seek First Amendment protection, then keep your religious dictate out of government affairs. The 'residual' taxpayer income to which you imply has yet to be determined; even if it did, the City—like all other jurisdictions—must decide what is best for all its residents, regardless of the handouts your special interest group bestows upon us. Besides, how can you be sure your 'God' condones the actions of the government? Perhaps it is best to keep the separation of church and state. I am not telling you how to worship, but I am assuring you that this council rules on laws that benefit all religious groups, not just the most influential."

Xavia approached the podium.

"I challenge Adamson to prove that Fermata Cellars is a doorway to Hell. Even if my alleged ghosts were to provide any sort of temptation, it is the responsibility of the seeker, not the business owner, to find a path toward righteousness. One's spiritual journey is reliant upon his or her actions and choices. We must take responsibility for our own actions.

"As for the accusation that Ms. Clark's death was our doing, we are greatly disturbed to hear of Edie's passing. Although she had opposing views of the City's land-use policies, she was a member of our human family and none of us ever wished her harm. If Reverend Adamson has any evidence to prove otherwise, I encourage him to submit it now. In the meantime, I assure you, none of us acted to snuff her out. Accusing any of us of wrongful death is tantamount to slander. We won't take lightly to such defamatory charges."

Xavia moved away from the podium.

"Does anyone else wish to address the Council?" Anza asked.

A well-groomed, middle-aged woman stepped forth.

"My name is Charlotte Smith. I was buying wine at Fermata Cellars few months ago when the lights flickered and I heard loud noises coming from the cellar. The cash register wasn't working properly and the staff became irritable with each other. The air in the room grew so thick that I started choking. And it was frightfully cold. I left without buying anything. I was too scared."

"Ms. Smith, are you a member of the First Church of Rivervine?" Mayor Anza asked.

"No, ma'am. I have never met Reverend Adamson or the Divinorums before. I read about this hearing in the newspaper and was compelled to tell my experience. This winery frightens me. There is something evil there and for the sake of all that is good in this world, we need to banish the demon."

"What demon?" Anza inquired.

"The one that is causing all this havoc."

"Have you seen this demon?"

"No, but I felt it."

"How do you know it's a demon?"

"I felt it, like a mother knows when her child's in danger. It's a sixth sense."

"But you didn't see any type of ghost or supernatural being?"

"I didn't need to. I sensed it."

"What evidence did this ghost leave behind?"

"My frightened nerves. To this day, I still have nightmares."

"Thank you Ms. Smith," Anza said, excusing the woman.

The next person to speak was a tall, well groomed, grey-haired man, wearing a nice blue suit and tie. When I got a look at his face, I noticed he was one of my instructors in college.

"Good evening Mayor Anza and members of the City Council. My name is Professor Todd Caprasen. I teach Anthropology at the University of California, Davis. The folklore surrounding the so-called 'Black Land' of Rivervine was the subject of my doctorate dissertation back in the late nineteen sixties before the Divinorums took title to the property. I know this area's history far better than Reverend Adamson. I would like to address several fallacies in his testimony, and present the facts behind the myths of Rivervine.

"In the early days of California, the Vitis River was a place where the pond turtles laid their eggs along the banks. Great blue heron fed at the water's edge. Black-tailed deer quenched their thirst after feasting on the wild grapes and oak twigs that grew in abundance. The Miwok and Maidu tribes met at the riverbank to trade their wares.

"In the 17th Century, the Mexican government sent Catholic missionaries to this area seeking to convert the indigenous people to the new religion. In their journals, the priests referenced a tribe called the 'Comatis' who made wine from the wild grapes and stored their vintages in a subterranean structure carved into the hill a short distance from the river's edge. The Catholics brought root stock of Mission grapes and began blending the native fruit with their own to produce the communal wine.

"Miwok and Maidu are part of a family of Penutian languages. Nowhere in their lexicon is there any word similar to 'Comati.' The word 'Comati' means 'peasant' in ancient Dacian— the language of the people inhabiting Romania prior to Attila the Hun's conquest in the 4th Century. There is no evidence of Romanian settlement as a significant contribution to California history prior to Statehood. Historians and anthropologists have yet to determine how the word 'Comati' became a reference the tribe of Indians settling in Rivervine before European or Chinese influence.

"Rivervine is also the only place in California history to reference winemaking before the Mexicans and Spaniards arrived.

"It was the English settlers in the 18th Century who dubbed this area with the name 'Rivervine' when they noticed the deer, raccoon, cougar and bear fed on the wild grapes encircling the trees along the river's bank.

"As with most pre-Abrahamic religions, Comati rituals involved dancing and chanting around a large pit of fire. They also practiced a form of spirituality that found mystic significance in the land, river and sky. But what made them different from other indigenous tribes was that Comati festivals were held at the cross-quarters between the seasons— instead of the solstices and equinoxes—and rather than invoking a supreme 'grandfather,' the Comati matron was the 'lady of the vines.'

"When the Russian immigrants came, they equated the 'lady of the vines' with their Baba Yaga—the crone in the woods.

"The Comatis met Captain John Sutter in 1841. The Austrian Catholic received a speculative land grant from the Mexican government to build New Helvetia—a saw mill community encompassing nearly forty-nine thousand acres headquartered in what is now Sacramento. Sutter's men set up camps along the Vitis River, harvesting the oak, cedar and pine.

"In January of 1848, Sutter's partner John Marshall discovered gold forty miles north of Rivervine, setting off what became known as the great California Gold Rush. Sutter ordered his men to tap the Vitis River for the precious metal. That August, a fire of unknown origin burned throughout the ninety-acre swath of land that we are discussing tonight.

"The land remained black and barren as immigrants from the Eastern United States, China, Italy, Ireland and other places came to Northern California to seek their fortunes. Whatever had caused the fire had also prevented new growth from rejuvenating or the layer of dark soil from eroding. Back then, anything involving fire and the color black was labeled 'Satanic.' Even today, as we have seen with testimony from the First

Church of Rivervine, religious excuses are difficult to challenge, even in the face of empirical evidence.

"Every culture throughout history has had some sort of religion, and every religion has deities representing good and evil. Humans fear what they don't understand. Whatever they fear, they label as evil. Since 1848, 'The Black Land' has been a mystery. Rumors have circulated as imaginations have crafted the folk history of the area. Each generation has passed rumors on to the next with every retelling of the story becoming more embellished and sensationalistic than the one before.

"Yet, development in the nineteenth century grew within the three acres southwest of the Black Land, becoming Rivervine's Mercantile District. There was a general store, barber shop, livery stable, butcher shop, hotel and saloon, as well as a few residences and boarding houses. The only person to build a home in the Black Land was an atheist physician named Dr. Ronaldo Castillo who built a one-acre health retreat in 1857 and lived there until he died of natural causes in 1902.

"When I commenced my analysis of the Black Land in 1967, I found the site to be completely fallow except for a cover of low-lying grasses and a lone weeping willow that stood at the edge of the riverbank—an anomaly for certain, as this species of tree is not indigenous to this part of the world. I found no native oaks, cottonwoods, rag weed, mugwort, blackberries or wild grapes that are commonly found in this region. I saw no rodent burrows, carcasses or other signs of animal activity—not even an empty beer can left by a wandering *Homo sapiens*. The soil itself was indeed black—the shade one would find after a recent controlled burn in a fire-prevention or weed-abatement operation. After checking with local authorities, I learned no scheduled burns had taken place here throughout the history of the fire department.

"I found no evidence of kerosene, gunpowder, arsenic, alcohol, or other propellant that would lead one to assume the fire was arson. I consulted experts in fire ecology, natural history, hydrology, chemistry, climatology, and other disciplines but none of them could explain how the land stayed so morbidly fallow and dark. Some pioneers' diaries referenced a knot on the willow that resembled a dragon's face, but this all goes back to humankind's attempt to explain what they do not understand, and demonize what they fear.

"After reading dozens of archived journals, talking to local historians, pouring over volumes of academic texts, and scouring every inch of the Black Land looking for evidence of some sort of occult activity, I found nothing conclusive. There were no markings on the walls of the semi-subterranean structure, no bloody tools, or skeletons resting in compromising positions.

"My studies of the soil found it to be looser and filled with more ash content than that the typical San Joaquin loam seen in surrounding properties. Such soil composition is enviable to wine-grape growers, but it is by no means evidence of some sort of curse by the devil. My entire dissertation became a study on how mass hysteria can lead to historical impertinence and the demonizing of nature.

"UC Davis awarded me my degree in 1969, the same year my friend Sage Divinorum returned from Vietnam. I encouraged him and his new bride, Xavia, to purchase this eighty-nine-acre parcel so they could find some peace after two years of war. Once they moved onto the property, the grapes, oaks, and cottonwoods began to rejuvenate. When I heard the news, I hurried back to Rivervine to investigate the new landscape. All I could deduce was that the fire of 1848 was caused by some sort of rare weather phenomenon that forced the vegetation into some type of shock-based dormancy to which introduced species such as weeping willows—which are indigenous to China—were resistant.

"I immediately ordered dendrochronological studies of tree-ring samples of the weeping willow. Results showed that it was indeed one hundred and sixty-nine years old, which supports the evidence found earlier that Chinese did have a presence in California prior to the Gold Rush, most likely as undocumented workers traveling on English ships coming from India.

"Another interesting element in this story is that the vines are not *Vitis californica*—the indigenous wild grapes of the Sacramento area. Rather, they are *Vitis vinefera*—the varietal used for making zinfandel wine.

"The large volume of anomalies regarding this property may certainly seem ominous, but as scientists, we cannot just blame it all on supernatural evildoing. There is still no empirical evidence that this Satan character actually exists, let alone is stalking the grounds of Old Town Rivervine.

"The word 'satan' is derived from the Aramaic Hebrew word for 'adversary.' The Hebrews created the character when they were enslaved by the Egyptians thousands of years ago. The Egyptians honored many gods, one of whom was named Set. His followers took the name Set-hen. The Hebrews used the image of Set to represent everything opposing their divine creator, Yahweh. If Yahweh was righteous, then Set was evil. If Yahweh's followers were to be obedient, humble and austere, then the Set-hens must be independent, self-confident and creative.

"The word 'devil' comes from the Greek 'diabolos' which means 'slanderer.' The New Testament of the Bible was written in Greek. If the only thing the Devil does is slander people, then Reverend Adamson must be a Satanist, because he has certainly slandered the owners of Fermata Cellars.

"As for the Divinorums and other merchants of Old Town Rivervine who self-identify as a group known as 'The Comatis,' the Comatis of Rivervine do not worship an adversarial deity that slanders anyone. They are animists who find spiritual relevance in the elements of land, river and sky. Instead of deities, they have Shining Ones—spiritual guides that lead them along the correct course of action. Such philosophy may not be Christian, but neither is it Satanic. They have never committed any crimes, and no harm has been done during any Comati celebration.

"The unexplained phenomena—electrical outages, emotional disturbances and whatnot—can all be chalked up to the power of belief. If we believe something to be true, we make it so. That is a common theme in any religion throughout history. This particular parcel has been rife with myths since the mid-eighteen-hundreds. As a professor of anthropology, I can tell you that a hundred and fifty years of myth building is impossible to assuage.

"Reverend Adamson and his false prophets are employing the same despicable tactics that the Inquisitors used centuries ago against alternative creeds. They are disseminating hysteria-causing propaganda accusing Comatis of the most hideous crimes and are wagering that their Big Lie will be repeated loudly and frequently enough to take hold of Rivervine's voters, consumers and taxpayers.

"I am appalled by the hypocrisy and slander used by the false prophets in order to build their megachurch, extort money from gullible parishioners, and force eminent domain against law-abiding land owners simply because the reverend covets their land.

"In parting tonight, I ask you to remember that gossip is not fact and neither is hysteria, even it wears a holy shroud. The Comatis are good, decent, law-abiding citizens. This witch hunt is an abomination of justice.

"Thank you."

"Thank you, Professor Caprasen." Mayor Anza dismissed him. "Is there anyone else?"

The last person to speak shocked us all. He was a man who always stood beside us at City Council meetings in the past.

"Good evening, everyone. I'm Vern Bradley. I own a cattle ranch on the other side of the vineyard. Most of you know me as someone who opposes government takeover of private land, but this case is different. I don't know anything about what that gentleman said about Satanism, but I can tell you ... I have seen the ghosts. I don't know about them being vampires, but they come and go in the blink of an eye. I hear talking late at night; and music, mostly a violin and some funny thing that kinda sounds like a banjo or a mandolin but different. It's a funny dressed man and woman—like Gypsies from the Old West. As soon as they see me coming, they disappear. They haven't done anything to harm me or my cows, so I never said anything before, but after hearing what I heard tonight, it's got me thinking.

"I'm a God-fearing man. I believe the Bible is the word of God. And right now, I think it might not be a bad thing to have these ghosts gotten rid of. That's all."

He tipped his hat and went back to his seat. Mayor Anza nodded.

"Has anyone here actually been bitten by any of these

vampires?" she asked.

No one stood up.

"Are there any ghosts in the room? If so, make the lights flicker or throw something across the room."

After waiting for a few seconds, nothing happened.

"If there are no other comments, I'll entertain a motion to close the public hearing."

"So moved," Josephson said.

"Seconded," White added.

"All in favor, say aye," Anza called out.

All four members yelled out, "Aye."

"Opposed?"

Silence.

The motion passed unanimously to close the public hearing and the Council began discussing the subject amongst themselves.

McCain, with his long, jet-black hair and gaunt figure, stood up and yelled, "I have seen the light. Reverend Adamson speaks the truth. Whoever denies his request will burn in Hell. I assure you all that I will not be among the damned. I motion to condemn the property and begin formal abatement procedures."

The entire room filled with commotion. Some cheered. Others booed. Whispers flew across the room as people mumbled to each other. Mayor Anza once again tapped the gavel several times calling for order in the chambers.

"I think Warner's right," White said. "To knowingly allow the public to enter a site that has been proven to cause health and life safety risks shows that it is a threat of some sort. We may not be able to prove the existence of ghosts or vampires, but we have enough evidence to conclude that something falling outside the scope of the Uniform Building Code is responsible for creating a public nuisance and safety hazard. I'll second the motion."

"Before calling for a vote among the Council, I would like to say a few things," Anza protested. "First of all, the Divinorums have been citizens in good standing with this community for thirty-four years. They have never been arrested. Their winery operations are all up to code. They and the other business owners of Old Town bring in revenue to the City. I agree with Ms. Divinorum that this will set a precedent, here in Rivervine and other locales. Are we going to abate Saint Bernadette's over the Crying Confessional on Christmas Eve? What about the historic buildings in the Mercantile District? I think this is all beyond ridiculous. Will there be any more discussion from the Council?"

The other four shook their heads.

Anza continued: "It's been moved by Vice-Mayor McCain and seconded by Council Member White to condemn the property and begin formal abatement procedures at Fermata Cellars. All in favor?"

The other two yelled out, "Aye."

"Since the mayor cannot vote while chairing a meeting, I'll pass the gavel to Vice-Mayor McCain."

She handed McCain the little hammer and uttered, "I vote no."

McCain stated the results: "Motion passes four to one. The property owners have ten days to appeal the decision with the superior court. If no appeal is filed, the City will then take title to the property on November twenty-eighth. The Divinorums will have until June 21, 2004 to vacate and abate the property.

As the meeting wrapped up, I heard Adamson muffle one last parting shot to Mayor Anza when she stepped down from the dais.

"You're nothing but a nigger spick dyke," he said. "You will rot in hell for your whoredoms."

"What a dick!" I uttered under my breath.

"I heard that, Mr. Chavez," Professor Caprasen chuckled.

"Hey! You remember me? It's good to see you again. I didn't know you knew Xavia and Sage."

"Yes, we've been chums since before the war. We lost touch after I got married and moved to Davis. When I heard about this hearing, I had to come."

"Well, thank you for speaking. Sorry these dipshits didn't listen to you."

"That's how it goes sometimes. We in the scientific community are accustomed to being heckled by our skeptics."

"What the hell is up with McCain? What was that all about?"

"I have no clue. That came straight out of left field."

Xavia and Sage walked up and wrapped their arms around their long-lost friend.

"Thank you, Todd," Sage said, his face still flush from stifling tears.

"I'm sorry, man," Caprasen answered. "What are you going to do?"

"We don't have the money to fight this in court. Adamson does. I guess we'll just wait it out."

"Care to come over for a glass of wine, Todd?" Xavia asked.

"Sounds wonderful," Caprasen answered. "We have a lot of catching up to do,"

"Manuel, would you like to join us?"

"Thanks, but I have a migraine. You three have a good

time."

As the trio walked away, I heard Caprasen mention to the Divinorums, "I see Zinfandel was on her best behavior tonight."

"Sometimes in war, you have to lie low and wait before striking," Sage murmured.

I went home and picked up the phone.

"Joaquin, can you come over? We got some horrible news tonight and I just need you to hold me."

"I'll be right there."

SAUIN

Friday, Nov. 7, 2003, 7:00 p.m.

Christine and Holly closed the winery today so I had time to leave work before the ceremony. Xavia scheduled our Sauin ritual for exactly five o'clock (sundown). We were all in somber spirits. This was going to be our last ritual together.

When I got to the Oppidum around 4:45 p.m., crimson and black ribbons greeted me. One black candle burned in the center of the altar along with Xavia's little stone Awen and Mrs. Rhoads' incense of rosemary, cinnamon, cloves and sage. On the left stood a carafe of wine. On the right was a plate of apple bread torn into bite-size pieces. Pine cones, dried pomegranates and crow feathers filled the rest of the space.

This time, we entered from the west side of the Oppidum as Xavia waved her smudge stick over us to cleanse our auras. We then walked counter-clockwise around the circle until the last person completed the round.

The chant itself was simple:

"On this night of summer's end, this invitation we extend, to the wise ones of the past, with your knowledge that is vast, guide us through these darkest nights and fill our vision with your sights."

We must have repeated it a dozen or so times. None of the Comatis played an instrument tonight, but I could have sworn I heard a violin and something that sounded like a medieval mandolin. At one point, I glanced over at the vineyard and spied a white misty cloud. The longer I gazed into the vines, the more defined the vision became. At first, all I saw was a bunch of animals gathered around the mist. There were deer, squirrels, a couple of raccoons and a fox. I squinted my eyes tighter and saw a faint image of an oddly dressed man playing an oddly shaped instrument. He made eye contact with me and nodded. Then he was gone. I never saw the violin player.

A few moments later, the chanting got louder and I could no longer hear the violin. The last note I heard was an E string go flat. I looked over at Lily, assuming she might have pulled out her instrument, but she was in the circle chanting with everyone else; her instrument was nowhere in sight.

I scanned the periphery of the circle and landed on Xavia with her hands extended toward the sky, eyes closed and chanting her heart out.

After the last round, she threw down her arms and head, and everyone stopped chanting. As she raised her head back up, she called out, "This is a night of transformation for us all. We stand at the crossroads of autumn and winter, torn between the happiness of life's splendor and the sadness of knowing a powerful oppressor seeks to destroy us. Do we plea to the ancestors for protection and strength, or ask them to guide our fortunes elsewhere? Let us now take a moment for them to respond. Close your eyes and let the ancient ones speak to your hearts."

This was the quietest I have ever heard this crowd.

I cheated, though. I squinted my right eye open just a tad. Erin Tuft stood five people away from me. Her arms stretched out and her head bent down slightly; her body leaned over and she barely balanced on the balls of her toes, as if something or someone were holding her up. I have no idea how she kept from losing her balance. After several moments, I could see her eyes well up and she nodded. Then she fell to the ground and started sobbing. Everyone snapped out of their meditations but no one reacted.

Xavia stepped over to Erin to help her up. Once the teen

got back in place, Xavia moved into the center of the circle and asked for everyone's attention.

"I believe our oracle tonight is found in our beloved Erin. Take a deep my breath, my dear, and tell us what you saw."

The youth huffed for a few moments, struggling to find her voice.

"Another great fire is coming," Erin announced, speaking in an unusually high pitch and shaky voice. "There is anger and vengeance in the flames. We all need to leave Rivervine by summer solstice. It's greater than Reverend Adamson and it will affect all of us, not just Fermata Cellars."

We all gasped and looked at each other with wide eyes. Xavia lowered her head, inhaled a deep breath, and exhaled an exasperated air of melancholia.

"Tell us more, dear one," Xavia interrogated.

"I don't know," Erin cried. "She just begged us to leave."

"Was it the Lady of the Vineyard—the one who told you to join the Army?"

"No. It was a Middle Eastern woman in a white gown, wearing a gold crown with a large bluish purple stone with gold flecks in the center. She didn't say her name, but our Lady left with her. They headed toward the vineyard."

We all looked to the south but saw nothing. The silence was broken as everyone talked amongst themselves.

"Does anyone else have a message from the ancestors or other Shining Ones?" Xavia called our attention back to the circle.

There was no response.

"Thank you, ancient ones for your wisdom. We ask for your assistance to help us understand this situation, heal the heartache and financial wounds, and triumph over our aggressor."

Everyone fell silent as the melancholy waved over the congregation.

"There is an answer," Xavia assured. "It may not be the response we want, but it will be what is best for our community."

She then nodded to Brigid to pass around the bread, and Lily to follow with the wine.

"This is our last feast as a community. Let us partake in merriment, and not let our oppressors rob us of our love and trust. The ancestors will guide us individually where we shall go from here. Take this, in remembrance of our tribe."

After the last person finished his communion, Xavia collected the plates and cups, and called out, "This rite is now ended. Let us go in peace."

The other Comatis left to partake in their potluck, although no one had much of an appetite. We had seven months to come up with a Plan B.

I ran up to the office to type this really quick. In the event I do not return, it is because I have decided to wander the vineyard in search of that man in the mist and find out once and for all who this Zinfandel character is.

Saturday, Nov. 8, 2003 3 a.m.

I walked over to the spot in the vineyard where I had seen the white mist. Once again, I heard the tinny mandolin-type music, this time without a violin accompaniment.

As I got closer, the cloud seemed to take the shape of a very tall, lean, dark-haired young man playing a wooden stringed instrument shaped like a tear drop with a broken neck. Although his image was translucent and barely recognizable, I could tell he looked sick—with sunken, slanted eyes and patchy, mottled skin. He frightened me. It wasn't the foreboding feeling I got from

Lily's van, though. I realized my fear was rooted in my own prejudice as I looked at his eyebrows and facial hair that grew in uneven patterns around the blisters that protruded from his pale skin. I took a deep breath and decided to break the ice diplomatically.

"What is that you're playing?" I asked, trying not to act like a dork.

"A cobza," he answered. "It is a Romanian instrument."

"That's really cool. By the way, my name is Manuel. What's your name?"

"Anton."

"Are you a vampire?"

Damn! I was bold. What the hell possessed me to ask that?

"Some may say."

"Why do people say you're a vampire?"

"I get sick when the sun touches my skin. In my family, we call it the 'crazy blood.' My uncle had it too. I am sorry if my ugliness frightens you. I really do not mean any harm. I just want to be left alone to play for my animal friends."

"Do you mind if I stay awhile and listen? Your music sounds wonderful. I really like it."

"Fine, pull up a patch of earth."

I plopped my ass down and spent the next half hour listening to him strum. A little fox came up and sat right down in my lap. As I stroked the creature's soft, plush fur, it dawned on me that I was with a potentially rabid wild animal and listening to a vampire ghost.

Still better than being in Chiapas.

Something happened though, after about the sixth or seventh tune. Anton got angry and threw his instrument down in a fit of rage. His outburst startled me and I flinched. The fox ran off.

"What's wrong?" I shrieked, fearing I had offended him somehow and wondering what he might do to me. My heart raced and fear paralyzed me.

"I am sorry," he said, calming down a little bit. "My hands do not want to cooperate. This crazy blood sickness that I have—the one that blisters my skin in the sun—affects my nerves and sometimes I cannot play. It does not matter anymore anyway. Tonight is my last night with the cobza. I am going to be reincarnated and will be rid of the crazy blood once and for all."

He held his head in his hands for a moment, and then looked up at me with a peaceful countenance on his face.

"I have to go," he sighed, picking up his beautiful stringed teardrop and handing it to me. "The cobza is yours. If you are going to be a Comati, you will need to learn to play an instrument. Since Lily has Vondella's fiddle, her best friend should have my cobza."

"Thank you," I replied. "But who is Vondella?"

"She is my sister. She was in circle tonight. Did you not see her?"

A rush of bile jetted up my gullet. Pieces of the puzzle were starting to come together.

"I heard a violin but I never saw one," I responded, hoping my discomfort wasn't too obvious.

"Well, she was my best friend, my only human friend; never missed a note. When her bow hit the strings, it was like listening to lightening—not the rattle of thunder, but the spark of electricity shooting across the starlit sky. There was a beautiful fury in her music, an unabandoned connection between her and the spirit of music. When we played together, the notes bonded us. Our midnight music time was the only part of my life that ever brought me any happiness. Even in death, we continued to play together. Now that I am reincarnating, I can no longer join her. But at least our instruments can stay with the tribe."

"Why are you going?" I asked.

"I hate being dead. I want a whole new body with a new future and no crazy blood. Thomas and Tanya have agreed to be my parents. I am so excited! When I am of age, I am going to ask Brigid to marry me!"

I wasn't sure how to process what I just heard. Reincarnation is real? People can pre-arrange who their parents and spouses will be? This is crazy!

"But Brigid will be almost eighteen years older than you," was the first thing to pop out of my mouth; an obvious knee-jerk reaction. "You're going to ask her to stay faithful to you that whole time? Put her life on hold for you? How does this reincarnation shit work anyway? What if you forget the deal and leave her an old maid?"

"The four of us have already reached an agreement. Worst case scenario is that Brigid devotes the next two decades to her music. Thomas and Tanya have the family they want, and I get a new physical shell that can dance in the sun."

"What about Vondella?" I inquired.

"She has made her own arrangements."

That was the end of our conversation. Anton was gone, not even the mist remained. But the cobza lay on the ground just as real as anything that was played on the stage at the Zinfandel Festival. I picked it up and headed towards my car. I put the instrument in the back seat, feeling honored that such an important figure in Rivervine folklore would bequeath to me his valuable heirloom.

But I didn't get in the car. Instead, I locked the doors and walked back to the tasting room.

When I got to the building, I took a deep breath and tried to ignore the hair on the back of my neck that was standing on end. I grabbed the key and unlocked the door to the tasting room, figuring if Erin Tuft could descend the dark flight of stairs to the wine cellar, so could I.

As I opened the door to the cellar, I went to turn on the light at the top of the stairwell. It wouldn't come on. I flicked the switch repeatedly—frantically—but still, not even a spark.

Oh shit!

Then, at the bottom of the stairs, an oil lamp appeared out of nowhere. My heart raced so fast that I could hear it throbbing like a sousaphone. A chilly breeze started to swirl around my feet, heading up to my face.

"Oh my God," I begged. "Please don't hurt me. I mean you no harm. I just want to talk about the winery. Please don't hurt me. Please don't hurt me!"

As I headed downstairs toward the lamp, I saw her—looking just as alive as I was, not transparent like Anton or Edie. She stood near the 1999 vintage of Requiem, wearing a crimson Victorian gown with a black bustier and black lace trim. She had a voluptuous Gypsy figure with the same slanted deep brown eyes and high cheekbones as Anton. Her long, wavy black hair cascaded across her shoulders as the notorious violin rested between her chin and right shoulder. The specter lifted her left arm and the bow crossed the strings as she started to play a most beautiful piece that I did not recognize.

She's left-handed.

What wonderful music—melancholy, yet seductive. The key of G minor had never sounded so ethereal. Her body waved back and forth in serpentine motions, reminding me of a cobra dancing to a snake charmer. Strangely though, her E string kept going flat—just like Lily's. It was the same sound I heard earlier tonight.

When she finished the piece, she put down her violin, flashed a flirtatious smile at me and spoke in a soft but firm tone of voice.

"Buenas tardes, Señor Chavez. ¿Como les puedo ayudar?"

Shocked at her ability to speak my old language, I returned the smile, albeit nervously. Our eyes met for a fraction of a second, but my anxiety forced me to look at the walls, then the floors—anywhere but directly into those cognac eyes. She halted as if noticing my nervousness and continued speaking in English.

"Step closer, darling. I will bring you no harm. I know you are afraid of me, but I assure you that I do not kill indiscriminately. All I ask is that you not turn on the electric light, please. It hurts my eyes. I much prefer the illumination of a single oil lamp. Not a candle, though; my energy tends to cause a draft that will quickly extinguish the flame. The chimney from the oil lamp offers far better protection against my inadvertent breeze."

So she doesn't kill indiscriminately' but she does kill discriminately? Good God, what am I facing here?

I couldn't get past that line, but I didn't have the courage to ask. Instead, my dorky mouth spewed the question: "You speak Spanish?"

She chuckled and answered, "I speak many languages— Spanish, English, Romanian, Russian, Penutian, Ohlone, Cantonese, German, Gaelic. Who knows? I might even learn Arabic one of these days."

Her eyes locked with mine—I felt her reading them, transcribing the graffiti written on my irises.

"Oh, and yes, I have killed people. I know that is what you really came here tonight to ask me. And yes, I am the vampire about whom Miss Fern is writing."

She paused for a moment and looked at me. Goosebumps pimpled my skin.

"Oh, poor darling, you're shivering," she consoled. "Here, put this on."

From out of thin air, she conjured a thick, dark-colored, wool cloak between her hands and wrapped it around me (I couldn't decipher the color in the poor lighting). I thanked her and began to feel a little calmer—but not much.

"You must be Zinfandel," I stated, again feeling like a dork. She was so gorgeous and formidable. My inferiority complex grew with each uncomfortable second that I stood there.

"My full name is Xin Vondella," she informed me. "My father was Chinese. His family name was Xin—X-I-N. In Asian cultures, the family name precedes one's given name. Vondella is the Comati word for 'precious girl.' Since I was the youngest of seven children and the only daughter, that was the name my parents gave me. Now I have a wine named after me."

"How did that come about," I asked. "I thought Zinfandel was an Italian varietal."

She chuckled again and set the record straight.

"When I was nine years old, a German horticulturist found himself lost in Comati territory. During his stay here, he developed a fondness for the wine we made. He also seemed to be quite taken with my precocious nature and love for performing. I would sing songs for him and dance in the silliest fashion."

Her eyes turned from mine and a scowl crossed her face. *This man did something inappropriate to her.*

A moment later, she shook off the stupor and continued her story.

"He kept calling me 'Zeinferdel.' When he returned to Germany, he took some of our vines and made a fortune selling his 'new grape' to the Italians and Croatians. Both groups claim title to the vine, but his first client was actually a man from Switzerland named Sooter."

She chuckled again and added, "So many people think Sooter came here to start a saw mill. What he really wanted was wine. But since trees were more plentiful than vines, he realized he could earn immediate cash if he started out in the timber industry while propagating the grape vines and waiting for them to mature."

"So what happened to the vines?"

"You are drinking them," she answered, conjuring a glass of wine and handing it to me. She continued her story.

"By the time I met Sooter, I was a beautiful nineteen-year-old girl, very popular among his New Helvetians. These men, mostly from the Eastern United States, enjoyed my dancing and fiddle playing. My sexual dexterity and lack of inhibition kept them plenty entertained. But they started treating me like one of the parlor girls back in Boston and I would not stand for that. They would get drunk and rowdy and lose control of their mouths.

"Nine years later, one of Sooter's men found gold in a river a little ways north of here. From then on, New Helvetia's economy relied more on placer mining than timber. More and more men arrived. They introduced me to an amber-colored wine called whiskey. Oh, how I loved it! They would offer me bottles of the luscious libation in exchange for sexual favors.

"At first, yes, I agreed to please them. There were so few

women among them that I felt sorry for these hard-working laborers. They deserved to feel the soft compassion of a woman's touch now and then. And I liked the attention they gave me in return. I also liked the whiskey. My father liked the opium.

"So we started a business. The prospectors paid us gold, whiskey and opium. My father managed the accounts. I provided the services.

"But jealousy set in among the men and no one wanted to share me. And to be honest with you, I did not like all of the prospectors anyway. Some were handsome. Others were ugly. Some were pleasant. Others were boorish. I wanted to handpick my lovers, not be subjugated to all of them all of the time.

"Soon they started hurling disrespectful, rude comments my direction, and trying to physically force me to be subservient to them.

"One night, when my father was lost in trance in his opium den, a prospector ordered me to cook him dinner. I told him to make it himself. He slapped me and then reached for his pistol."

Vondella turned her gaze toward the floor and paused for a moment. Her eyes grew large as she continued reminiscing.

"Before he could fire, I bent down, spun around, lifted my leg and kicked the gun out of his hand. When I regained my balance, I used my arm as a spear, driving my arrowhead-like fingernails into his throat. I then lunged against him, knocking the bastard down. He was too slow to react. I already had him pinned to the floor."

Her countenance went from pensive to maniacal.

"Noticing the scarlet juice against his white skin, I had to feed. Once I smelled the savory blood seeping from his neck, I could not resist lapping it up. My licks turned aggressive and started suckling the life force right out of him. His essence shifted from the incarnate realm to the discarnate one. Soon, there was nothing left. No blood, no breath.

"Realizing no one would defend me, I hid in my wine cellar. A few hours later, the scent of smoke wafted in the air and the walls steamed from the heat. Not knowing anything about fire behavior in a closed environment, I opened the door in hopes of rushing through the flames the way we would during a grass fire. But the back draft flared toward the bottles of alcohol. The last thing I saw was a flash of light. By morning, I could not see, hear, taste, smell or feel anything. I realized I was dead.

"It took me awhile to gather my wits. What was I going to do if I had no physical senses? I meditated on the issue, remembering all the Taoist lessons my father taught me about chi and the movement of energy. It was then that I was able to home in on my surroundings. I sensed the ruins of the cellar and the entire vineyard covered in ashes. The fire destroyed my heart more than my body. Without a physical shell, I had no way of knowing how to move. I could not communicate. I could do nothing but wonder what was happening to me.

"All the memories of this place ran through my mind. I thought of my school days as a student of good ol' Father Kristobal who taught me how to read and write—his lessons on history and science. He showed me how to think, not just what to think. I saw visions of him meeting my father who was the only Chinese person Kristobal had ever seen. He ended up staying with my family.

"But now we are all discarnate. Father Kristobal, my brother Anton, and I are the only ones who communicate with the incarnate realm on a regular basis. Anton plays his cobza for the creatures of the night. Father Kristobal stays close to his beloved little Basque girl. I have always been the Lady of the

Vineyard.

"Father Kristobal's lessons always took place in the wine cellar that was once in this exact location. That is why I protect it so fervently. This is my wine cellar. Nobody attacks it and survives. I may not be able to save the world, but I can rescue this minuscule scrap of it. This is where I was born, schooled, and killed. I am not leaving."

Trying to keep my wits about me and repress the story she just recounted, I shrugged off her last statement and moved on to my next question.

"What did you tell Glenda Fern that has her acting so strangely?"

"I need a scribe to chronicle my life," Vondella guffawed. "She has the gift of storytelling and an understanding of the dark mysteries. She also knows the true meaning of a vampire."

"What exactly is that truth?" I asked point blank, fearing her response. She chuckled before answering.

"Vampires are not converted by some outside influence as so many of your modern folktales would have you believe. I could bite you here and now and leave you with nothing but a scar; you would never rise from the dead and become immortal. All those myths were fabricated by scribes selling their stories to gullible readers. The truth is vampires are born with a mutant form of chi—the multifarious vital life force energy that makes up the universe. A vampire's chi registers on the lower end of the spiritual spectrum, making it sensitive to bright light, high-pitched noise, and hot temperatures. This form of sensory deprivation heightens our physical and psychic powers though, which is what makes us appear super-human. We can exist in either the incarnate or discarnate realm, just like anyone else. As incarnates, we are human, so we can be killed by any means that would end the life of another *Homo sapiens*. As discarnates, we are ghosts who can be banished—given the correct form of exorcism. Silver bullets, steaks driven through our hearts and the separation of our heads from our shoulders are myths scribes use to sell their vampire-slaying propaganda."

This news intrigued me. It all made sense, but there was one thing I still wondered about.

"Where does the blood fetish fit in?"

"Blood is the source of chi. When we are weak, we must replenish our energy by feeding via sanguinary means—usually the meat of a cow, deer, elk or other form of red-meat will suffice; white meat animals do not have as high a potency of chi after slaughter as red meat animals do. Vampires do not need human blood to satiate our needs, unless our weakness is so great that only our own kind can save us."

"Xavia said she has fed you. What did she mean by that?"

"When my energy is dangerously low, usually during the summer, I can feed from a woman's menstrual flow. Xavia was my source before she became a crone—what Comatis call a woman who is past menopause."

That answer grossed me out completely. The thought of Xavia having oral sex during her period—with a female ghost no less—was one image I had to put out of my mind, so I continued my questioning.

"What's going on at the summer solstice? Why do we have to leave?"

Vondella chortled.

"Adamson thinks he can banish us, but he has a surprise awaiting him. That is why Inanna told Miss Tuft the Comatis need to leave by the summer solstice.

"Who is Inanna?"

"She is my original teacher, before Kristobal. She is the one who taught me the ways of the marsh, six thousand years ago."

"What do you mean?"

"Let me start from the beginning. I spent my first physical incarnation as a pit viper living in the marshes of what is now known as southwestern Asia. My favorite pastime was to spend the day entwined in the branches of a pomegranate tree. I loved this tree so much that I blessed its fruit with all the talents Inanna had taught me. Any creature that consumed the luscious red juice would be filled with her knowledge, vivacity, and dexterity.

"Back then, people looked to the trees and animals for guidance in their spiritual affairs. We snakes were not cursed because we were predators who moved elegantly. Humans knew we never killed for sport, greed, or spite. We killed for survival, using the talents with which nature blessed us.

"But we were not just deadly. We were strategic, seductive—symbols of strength, wisdom and perseverance. Serpents do not waste their days seeking innocent victims to kill mercilessly. We make love. We dance. We care for our young and protect our homes. We gather in merriment and ponder the meaning of life. Our days are filled with happiness, passion, debate, grief, rage—the same emotions that affect humans. We are not merely angry, vindictive villains with nothing better to do than cause harm to simple passersby.

"There was one day, though, that started the downward spiral away from the wisdom of nature. I befriended a young woman whose mate became jealous of our relationship. I had taught her to be self-assured and independent. I encouraged her to think for herself. We grew to become close friends.

"Her mate did not approve of our relationship. He wanted

her to be subservient and obedient to him—without questioning anything he asked of her. When she stood up to him—a result of my influence on the poor girl—he devised a ridiculous story about me being a sneaky, evil temptress with a plan to ruin all of mankind. There was no evidence to support his theory, but the woman was so in love with this man that she believed his hearsay and refused to speak to me again. He took his bride and left the marsh. I never saw her again.

"His ruthless gossip expanded throughout the marsh. The other predators refused to share their hunt. The river receded when I came to drink. My own pomegranate tree shook me off its branches. I starved to death. So did the other vipers of my species. We became extinct.

"Over the next six millennia, my image was painted as a ferocious creature with superhuman powers and a plan to take the Earth away from the precious Divine Male. This husband and other supposedly infallible prophets gave me a mutilated man's image so that I would not be perceived a spindly, wistful animal unable to defend herself against the ever-so mighty man. They stole my beauty and elegance, and reduced the truth of my existence to an angel so vain that I was cast out of heaven. Inanna had no means to defend me."

As she spoke these words, I was overcome with the realization of just exactly who I was talking to and why everyone was so afraid of her. She was the original Satan—the antichrist herself. Yet, I was caught between wanting to believe her story and wondering if everything she told me—about her history, victimization, and everything else—was a lie used to sway me from the path of righteousness. What if she really was the devil? I was standing there alone completely vulnerable to the caprice of an invincible specter who bragged—without any hint of remorse—about committing murder. My stomach turned sour and I wanted to vomit right where I stood. My heart raced faster than any night I ever stayed up drinking coffee while studying for finals. Every limb in my body shook. My mind went numb. I dropped to my knees and wept profoundly. She knelt beside me and wrapped her arms around my shoulders.

"My apologies, darling. I did not mean to frighten you. It is just that you are the first incarnate other than Glenda or the Comatis to listen to my story. Perhaps my passion got the best of me. Please, realize that I will not harm you. Everything I have told you is the truth. I have admitted everything and omitted nothing. My hope was that you would realize the damage caused by spiritual character defamation. In no way did I intend to appear cantankerous. I have so much pain and anger penned up inside me. Please understand."

I shook harder than I had all evening. My mind raced trying to rationalize everything, but my nerves kept getting in the way. My breathing hastened and it was getting harder to avoid vomiting. I empathized with her side of the story, but two-and-a-half decades of theological upbringing, was difficult to undo. How could I just throw away everything I had been taught, and accept her story as truth? Surely I would rot in Hell for this. But what if everything she said was true and everything I had been taught was a lie? I thought about the horror of the crusades and the witch trials. I thought about Rome and Constantine's deceptive role in converting the Pagans to the new religion. I remembered what this country's founding fathers did to Christianize the Indians and the African slaves. This entire scenario had me wondering where to find the answers.

With tears streaming down her face, the strong, independent, self-professed whore offered me a reassuring embrace. Despite her distressed countenance, she focused on *my* misery and told me, "I know someone with whom you need to speak. Go to Saint Bernadette's. Your answers will be found there."

I was truly perplexed. Why would the devil tell me to go to church? I immediately thought of every religious-based horror movie I'd ever seen. Images of defecation and sacrilege ran through my mind. What on God's green earth did she have planned? But then I thought, where else could I go for salvation? Who else could I trust if not the priest who christened me? The nausea was too much. Before I could lose the entire contents of my stomach, Vondella firmly grabbed my shoulders, looked me in the eye and insisted, "Go to Saint Bernadette's ... or your orange tree—wherever you like."

I turned to her, completely perplexed, and asked, "You know about the orange tree?"

Vondella lowered her eyes and answered, "Yes. I am the racer snake you have befriended."

That was it. I couldn't stand it anymore. This was too much for me to absorb for one evening. My breathing hastened even more and my entire body shook. I couldn't look her in the eye.

Vondella noticed my level of anxiety and apologized.

"I have upset you enough tonight. I must leave you now."

She disappeared. I ran out of the cellar and headed to my car, hopped in, hit my foot on the accelerator, and drove toward Saint Bernadette's. I passed the orange tree, stopping only for a second, long enough to conjure images of a Satanic snake handing me the beautiful lines of the poem I wrote for Brigid last February.

When I arrived at the church, I knew full well the doors would be locked. But I still hoped that maybe by happenstance,

Father Armando would be out for a midnight stroll. Or maybe just being on the steps of the church would comfort me. Perhaps the janitor would have forgotten to lock the doors and I could get in long enough to light a novena candle and pray every Catholic prayer I've learned since childhood. I didn't care. I tugged onto every last aspect of hope I had. When I got to the lot, I parked my car, ran up the stairs, and found the doors shut tight.

I fell to the ground and cried.

My stomach finally caved to the stress and I vomited right there at the top of the steps. I cried even harder knowing that I made such a disrespectful action to a church I loved with all my heart. I cried so hard that my soul filled with inebriation.

Somewhere in the midst of my stupor, someone found me. I felt a reassuring hand touch my shoulder and immediately, my tears vanished.

I froze, staring at the pool of vomit, repulsed by the odor and embarrassed at the realization that whoever's hand was on my back could see and smell the vomit too. Awashed in shame, I hastily whispered, with tears in my voice, "O my God, I am heartily sorry for having offended Thee, and I detest all my sins, because I dread the loss of heaven, and the pains of hell; but most of all because they offend Thee, my God, Who are all good and deserving of all my love. I firmly resolve, with the help of Thy grace, to confess my sins, to do penance, and to amend my life."

The hand patted me on the back. I heard the unrecognized voice of a man say, "I absolve thee of all sin in the name of the Father, Son and Holy Ghost."

At that moment, I was encompassed by an overwhelming sense of warmth and liberation. I looked down at the spot where

I had vomited and noticed it was gone. Not even the foul stench remained. Then I slowly looked over my shoulder and saw that it was not Father Armando, the janitor or any vagrant standing behind me. It was instead, a tall, dark-haired man wearing a long black robe and a large, wooden crucifix around his neck—not the vestments worn by contemporary priests. He offered me his hand to help me to my feet. Then he put his arm around me and we walked toward the locked doors, which he managed to open with just a wave of his hand.

As I stared into his eyes, I realized that this was no priest of the Sacramento diocese. I had just received absolution from the same man—or ghost, or saint or whatever—who taught Vondella how to read and wept in the confessional every Christmas Eve. My eyes welled up and my entire body felt as if it had separated from the earthly plane. I could tell my spirit was reaching the end of one incredible journey, while preparing for an expedition that was yet to come.

We entered the narthex, crossed ourselves with holy water, turned on the lights, and headed toward the sanctuary. We sat in one of the pews and began chatting like longtime fishing buddies.

"Are you Father Kristobal?"

He nodded and smiled with a soft-spoken, "Yes."

Something about him made me feel truly at ease. I had this irresistible urge to honestly open up to him and ask him all the questions I've always wondered.

"You were excommunicated from the church. Why are you still here when the church turned its back on you?"

He lifted his chin, smiled, and answered, "Ah. Now it is my time to confess. I was never excommunicated from the church. In fact, I was never an ordained priest, or even a parishioner. I am just a ghost.

"I travel all over the place. I love music and I love wine. I go wherever the music takes me. But my grapes are rooted in Rivervine. So I always find my way back here at some point. They are my first love ... well, second love."

He conjured a strange-looking horn instrument that was made of wood and bulbed at the end—like an early version of a clarinet, but much higher pitched and with a middle-eastern twang. He played it for a brief moment. I didn't recognize the tune, but it sounded like something you'd hear while belly dancers spun around and gyrated. When he finished his performance, he laid his instrument on the pew.

"I left Rivervine for a while, but came back when Xin Vondella was born because I knew the family was going to face trouble. Her greatest grandparents—Doina and Radu, and the generations after them—cared for my grapes so well that I could not let all their hard works go to waste. So I blended in with Luis Arguello's missionaries and somehow managed to convince them to end their missions at Sonoma and leave Rivervine alone. As for Saint Bernadette's, I stay here because I love the sacred mysteries. They are not made by the men who run the church government. They are not found in dogma, doctrine, recited prayers, or hymns. They are part of nature. They are part of me. I cannot deny my connection to them. They are what all seekers aspire to learn. Mystics, prophets, sages, clerics, holy men and women of all religions have always thirst to find those mysterious forces that meld the world of the known with the world of the unknown. My journey has led me here—for now.

"In my previous lives, I have been a monk, a Druid, a Templar and a Freemason. But the Catholic Church is my home because I love Her. She was the one who cleared my path so that

I could open myself to the sacred mysteries.

"You knew Saint Bernadette?" I asked.

He chuckled, but answered, "Oh no. Armando chose the name because he is Basque and Bernadette is a Basque saint. Bernadette visits here from time to time, but she mostly stays in her homeland. She is a sweet kid. The name of the church meant nothing to me so long as I was allowed to stay. Armando is a good man. He even puts up with my Christmas Eve antics."

My mind was so full of questions but my mouth seemed to be completely paralyzed. Father Kristobal just smiled and answered my questions anyway, as if he could read my mind.

"Manuel, my child, I've been watching over you since you were a fetus in your mother's womb. Your mom was such an amazing girl. I helped her get across the border when she was a teen. I knew if she could just find work in the California agricultural industry, she'd be all right. I also knew that Xavia and Sage needed help in the vineyard. It seemed like a good match."

The wheels in my mind started spinning and I was able to piece together the mysteries surrounding this character.

"My mother was fourteen when you met her," I told him, trying not to sound too accusatory. "Biblical scholars believe that Mary was fourteen when she gave birth to Jesus. Bernadette was about that age when the Virgin appeared to her at Lourdes. What is it about you and fourteen-year-old girls?"

He answered pensively: "Long ago, when the Romans ruled Palestine, I was a traveling musician wandering through the Jewish tetrarchy of Galilee. One of my favorite stops was the city of Nazareth where the most amazing woman lived. She was young, with child, unwed and terrorized by the religious leaders of her village for being headstrong and full of verve; she stood her ground against any elder who dared put her in her place. She would often stop by my little corner of the street to say hello and dance to the music I played on my mizmar."

As he said the word 'mizmar,' he picked up the fancy instrument and played a small tune before continuing his monologue.

"She said my music was the only reprieve she had from the stress of her terribly oppressed life. We had many conversations about philosophy, spirituality, morality and just about anything else intellects would discuss. We truly connected on a deep level.

"And she was so lovely. I would inhale her essence as if I were sniffing roses. She was soft and delicate to look at, but strong and invincible when confronted by her adversaries. Women back then were not allowed to be bold; they had to be docile and submissive. She was the first woman I ever met who could be simultaneously feminine and audacious. How could I avoid losing my heart to such a woman?

"I repeatedly begged her to join me. I imagined her dancing and singing while I played music. Her response was always no. Even though she longed to be free to live the life of a traveling minstrel, she had a visceral instinct guiding her along a different path.

"When rumors of her pregnancy became common knowledge, she accepted an offer of marriage from a carpenter. Naturally I was heartbroken, but I understood that he could provide for a family much better than a traveling minstrel could. He was a good man, but nonetheless it was difficult for me to watch someone I cared about so much wrap herself in arms that were not mine. The night she left with him, I took my own life. I sailed a boat onto the Sea of Galilee and threw myself overboard. My body lay at the bottom of the deep waters, but my spirit could not leave her. I loved her so much that even in the afterlife, I watched over her, frequently crossing between the incarnate and discarnate realms.

"Shortly after my death, the vain Tetrarch, Herod Antipas crossed her path. He became enamored with her and insisted she join his harem. My beloved refused. She and the carpenter were banished from the Tetrarchy. The carpenter had family in the city of Bethlehem, which was in the province of Judaea and outside of Herod's jurisdiction. So they headed south.

"Despite my jealousy toward the carpenter, I knew my beloved was better off with him than with Herod. I managed to hide the couple behind an invisible veil the Tetrarch could not pass. I kept them safe for a while, but there was only so much I could do.

"The Hebrew month of Tishri was upon us and everyone in the Jewish world was celebrating Rosh Hashanah. The baby was not due until Kislev two months later, but after several days of riding on a donkey, the bumpy ride forced my beloved to go into premature labor somewhere between Jerusalem and Bethlehem. None of the innkeepers in either town had a vacant room. As her contractions started coming at regular intervals, I realized I had to act quickly. My Turkish friend Nicholas knew the territory better than I, so I called to him in a dream. He informed me of a cave nearby that was home to a wayward lamb. When I asked him if the beast would mind sharing its abode with this family, he replied, 'The animal decided to allow it so long as the couple acted with respect.'

"My beloved and her husband agreed to be kind and grateful guests."

The padré finally paused.

Wow. This was certainly a different take on the story from anything I had learned growing up.

Once I was finally able to absorb it all, I had to ask, "So who were the three kings?"

"A trio of magi were known for their healing abilities," he answered. "Nicholas begged each of them to travel to Judaea to help this poor woman and child. The men packed their camels with their trinkets and herbs and headed for the cave. They were all astronomers well versed in the patterns in the nighttime sky, so that is where I kept my vigil—appearing as a giant blue star guiding them to the place where the lamb had offered its hospitality.

"The men arrived safely and were able to rescue my beloved, filling the cave with smoke burned from frankincense resin to prevent infection, and rubbing her cervix with myrrh oil to keep the perineum from tearing. They also lay golden bands across her belly to ease her pain. Several hours later, the most beautiful baby boy was born. Neither he nor his mother had any sign of infection or other health concerns.

"I thanked the men for their generosity. Nicholas made sure they returned home free from Herod's vengeance. He also gave each of them a bottle of brandy for their troubles.

"Many years passed. I continued watching over the family. It was difficult seeing my beloved live so happily with another man, but the most pain I ever suffered was witnessing the agony in her eyes the day her son died in a political battle waged in the name of righteousness.

"At age thirty-three, my beloved's son had grown to become just as headstrong and outspoken as his mother. The Roman regime did not take too kindly to the political dissenter— neither did the Jewish clergy. Both groups called him a traitor—a grievance punishable by death.

"There was nothing I could do to save him. I begged him

to run away before the guards could arrest him, but he refused my assistance, saying, 'I would rather die with my mouth open than live with it shut.'

"There he was, tortured under abject humiliation until the last drop of blood trickled out of his broken skin. The eyes of the woman I loved gorged with tears. I felt so helpless. There was nothing I could do to heal his wounds or her broken heart. All I could do was promise her I would do everything I could to prevent other mothers from enduring this type of trauma.

"In the centuries since my death, I had reincarnated as a Druid, a Templar Knight, and finally as a priest. But my beloved never called in the favor until almost seventeen hundred years after we last spoke face-to-face. She was once again caught in the middle of a political and religious struggle. This time, it was far north of our homeland. A tiny Pagan village in Romania was the battleground among the Catholics, Orthodox Christians, and Muslim Turks.

"The discarnate watching over the village was a Fifteenth Century Wallachian prince by the name of Vlad Tepes. During his lifetime, he had been raised Orthodox, but married a Hungarian Catholic girl after her father had financed his campaign to become ruler."

"Holy shit!" I screamed. "Forgive my language, Father, but are you talking about Prince Dracula?"

"Yes, my son," he answered. "The famous warlord never truly died. He became a vampire, much like Vondella and Anton whom you met earlier this evening."

"So what does he have to do with Rivervine?"

"The raided village was home to Zinfandel's greatest grandparents, Doina and Radu. I foresaw the confrontation, and sent some Anglican allies to mediate. They could not save the entire village, but my friends offered the captors three gold coins as ransom for themselves and the peasant couple.

"My Anglican associates brought the couple to Massachusetts, but once the Witch Trials hit, they could no longer offer Doina and Radu safety. It was up to me to get them out of harm's way. So, I brought them to Rivervine ... to become progenitors of a new race—the Comatis.

"Our journey to Rivervine is a blur in my memory. I just remember wandering ... and wondering. Finally, I was in a place where the landscape boasted magnificent grapes growing alongside beautiful, majestic oak trees. Giant elk roamed all over, and a river rushed through the area—sometimes soothing and calm, other times formidably rapid. Something about this location allowed me to find peace. It became my sanctuary. I knew this was where Doina and Radu should settle. So we made wine and built a cellar in which to store it.

"When the Catholics came here in the twentieth century, they brought with them the essence of my beloved. They built a church and named it after another young female outcast."

"Saint Bernadette!" I called out, just like a kindergartner yelling out an answer in class.

"Yes," he confirmed. "So here I am two millennia after my first encounter with the Nazarene angel, at Saint Bernadette's Catholic Church in Rivervine, California. This is the one place where I can feel her presence."

He paused for a moment, losing himself in thought.

I interjected: "You obviously love Mary more than anyone, to go through extremes like this."

"I keep my word to the best of my ability, although I cannot save all the wayward girls of the world. I managed to bring your mother here in the late nineteen seventies, but I will never forgive myself for letting my dear Vondella succumb to the fire in 1848, and I cannot save her from Reverend Adamson in 2003."

He hung his head down for a moment, then looked up at me and pleaded:

"Please Manuel, for me, so that I can compensate for my inadequacy more than one hundred and fifty years ago, please help me. I have no one else to turn to. I am not strong enough to battle Reverend Adamson. He is going to kill Vondella's spirit and destroy our vines forever. I have done everything I could to protect them, but now, I am defenseless. He is a very powerful and influential man. He is handsome, cunning, articulate and persuasive. Most of all, he is one of them—an incarnate. And he plays to the fears the populace has toward those of us on the other side. The people will never listen to us. But you are flesh and blood. They will listen to you."

"So what is my penance tonight?" I dared, "To go up against the original sinner? Couldn't I recite some Hail Marys and Our Fathers instead?"

"Prayer without action means nothing," he refuted. "We are not referring to your homosexual relationship or your mother's abortion denying you a sibling. Once again, religion and politics have proven themselves to be lousy bedfellows. This time, the entire Comati legacy stands to be extinguished."

"So what do I do?"

Conspicuous silence befell the room. Kristobal closed his eyes, bowed his head and folded his hands in front of his heart. As he whispered chants in a language I did not recognize, my eyes searched the room for another source of divination.

I did not like the answer my inner voice gave me.

"No, no, not Chiapas, you can't make me go there," I

pleaded.

"There is nothing you can do for Rivervine at this point," Kristobal muttered. "Go forth and ensure this fate does not befall another culture. I believe your friend Joaquin could use some help in his missions. In the name of the Father, Mother, Son, and Holy Ghost, this rite has ended. Let us go in peace. Amen."

The padré disappeared.

"¡Mierda!" I called out under my breath.

I drove home, took out my rosary and walked out into Mr. Fermanski's rose garden. This time, when I prayed "Holy Mother full of grace," the image in my mind's eye was not the fragile flower so many associate with her. Tonight, I pictured a big-boned, thick-skinned warrioress with a heart of gold.

I kissed my crucifix and stared at it for a little while. As I gazed upon the plastic figure, it dawned on me just how we're all related—Catholic, Orthodox, Pagan, or any other religion. I don't care anymore how people choose to label themselves. We're all part of this great mystery. What the actual truth is, who's to say? Every religion believes it's the one true religion. If truth is universal, why don't any of the so-called prophets agree with one another?

If Jesus is reading this right now, tell me where to go from here. I am so confused. I feel at peace for some dumb reason, but I'm still bewildered. I want to hear the answer from You, not an evangelical minister or racer snake. I need some sort of road map—the one absent from the orange leaf nine months ago. Otherwise, I'll be nothing but a disoriented fool taking directions from a fraudulent commander.

"I don't want to go to Chiapas," I spoke out loud. "That place sucks big, green donkey dicks."

"And it will continue sucking big green donkey dicks until someone like you intervenes," an invisible woman's voice told my inner ear.

Shocked at the vulgarity, I called out, "Mary?"

The woman's voice chuckled and responded, "I do not think Mary knows what a 'dick' is. I doubt she could have seen it from the donkey she rode to Bethlehem on."

Infuriated at the sacrilege, I screamed, "Vondella!"

If there is such a thing as psychic eye roll, I sure as hell felt it.

Friday, Nov. 14, 2003 5:30 p.m.

I no sooner got home from work today and the phone rang. It was Joaquin.

"Did you file the appeal?"

"No. We're not going to fight."

"Why the hell not? This is bullshit!"

"We know, but Adamson has money and we don't. Besides, there's more to the story. I can't talk about it."

It wasn't that I was forbidden from discussing the details. I just didn't know how to tell him about the planned summer solstice exodus. I never told him about the ghosts I talked to on Sauin either. All this esoteric stuff is just too weird and I didn't want to frighten him off.

"Well, if you're not busy tonight, the band's playing at Trails again. I'd love to see you in the audience."

"I could use a drink. Eight o'clock?"

"As always, there's a five-dollar cover charge but I can put you on the guest list. See you then!"

He hung up.

Saturday, Nov. 15, 2003 2 a.m.

Joaquin is asleep in my bed. He looks so beautiful and angelic. I am so in awe over my feelings for that man. We made love tonight. Every time he starts to go a little too fast or rugged, he notices me wince and immediately slows down and takes it easy. I want so badly to please him and I'm terrified that he'll leave me because I can't keep up with his stamina.

That's not the only thing keeping me from catching any winks. I'm tasked with selling off our current inventory. Since there's no reason to keep any of the winemaking equipment, Sage is trying to find someone to take it off his hands. Harvest just ended and we're left with tons of grapes to get rid of too.

Word's gotten out about the City Council condemning the land. Gawkers have packed the tasting room every day wanting to sample our "haunted wine." We've also received our fair share of death threats from those who don't think God works fast enough.

Joaquin just woke up and noticed I'm not in bed. I better get back.

Monday, Nov. 17, 2003 4:30 p.m.

This is normally my day off but Xavia and Sage called me in to discuss their meeting with Mayor Anza. They didn't look happy, but at least things aren't as bleak as they could have been. Xavia handed me a bunch of documents.

"As of November twenty-eighth, Fermata Cellars will be owned by the City of Rivervine," she said. "Carmelita made a deal with the rest of the Council to grant us squatters rights until June twenty-first of next year."

The City hired an independent appraiser who showed the current value as:

- Land $130,000
- Structural improvements $500,000
- Growing crops $110,000
- Business property $90,500
- Fixtures $1,000,000
- Total = $1,830,500

"Since the place is haunted, the cost of the 'nuisance' is the full value," Sage uttered, his voice sullen and dropped by a good two octaves. "The City's giving us nothing. Carmelita tried to bargain for us to at least get the value of the fixtures and business property, but the other four council members refused. The only sympathy they showed was allowing us to stay through summer solstice to deplete our current inventory and try to make alternative living arrangements.

"Knowing that Adamson has his eyes on the property, she made sure the provision stated, 'Said right shall be irrevocable by any party purchasing the property from the City,'" Xavia added.

"So, now what do we do?" I asked.

"I'm in the mood for pizza," Xavia offered. "Why don't we grab a bite to eat and a pitcher of beer? There's probably a football game on TV. That'll be a good distraction."

Tuesday, Dec. 2, 2003 8 a.m.

I just got in to work and heard the news: Adamson bought the property from the City for two hundred thousand dollars in cash yesterday. At least the City made good on its promise to place conditions on the sale that the Divinorums be granted squatters rights thru June 21, 2004.

"This property is worth almost two million dollars and he's getting it for ten percent of its value?" I yelped. "What a charlatan! And the City's giving us nothing? This just reeks with political corruption."

"Yes, it does," Sage replied. "But it's time for us all to move on. Brigid's going to college in San Francisco. Xavia and I are going to move down there with her. We'll find work somewhere. Worst case scenario, we can play music on the street corners if we have to."

"We're having a meeting tonight with the other merchants," Xavia chimed in.

9 p.m.

The meeting this evening was melancholy. Everybody's making plans to sell their property and move. We talked about staying nearby or leaving the area all together. Consensus was reached that we all wanted to go where nobody had ever heard of Comatis or "the haunted winery."

"So what's going to happen to our little family, our community?" Nadine asked.

"We'll have to keep in touch by email," Dr. Frank answered. "We can start an Internet group. Or heaven forbid, we should call or visit each other."

We all walked away sad and depressed. I called Joaquin as soon as I got home and invited him over.

"Let's do this." I said. "Let's go to Chiapas and fight for freedom. Let's make it our day jobs."

"Are you sure?"

"I've had three weeks to think it over. Let's go. Let's spend winter in Mexico. But I want one last Christmas in Rivervine."

"Alrighty then."

Thursday, December 25, 4 a.m.

Joaquin and I went to Midnight Mass at Saint Bernadette's.

He's been such a comfort to me these past weeks. He even offered to let me move in with him. Xavia and Sage have both assured me I can keep working at Fermata Cellars until I sell the entire inventory.

We got to the church plenty early. Christmas Eve is always packed at Catholic masses, but Saint Bernadette's is especially full because everyone wants to see the Crying Confessional. This year has me particularly interested now that I know whose voice is doing the weeping.

I stopped by the Novena altar. As always, there were two types of candles available—an itty bitty votive for one dollar, and a seven-day candle encased in glass for three dollars.

This will be the last wick I ever light here. Better make it a big one.

I put three bucks in the offering slot—not having any clue what to pray for, so I just said, "Here's to ... whatever. It's in Your hands now, God."

We found a seat near the choir and waited for mass to begin. It was the same scene as every other year: We sat through the usual scripture reading and sang all the same carols. The kids were cute reenacting the nativity scene. Father Armando wrapped up the Eucharist. Then the media frenzy hit—all the reporters prepped their cameras and digital recorders in the hopes that Saint Christopher soon would be there.

Once the crying began, the doors of the narthex flung open and everyone saw the snow storm blowing outside. The votives at the Novena altar all blew out, but the seven-day candles encased in glass remained lit.

It never snows in Rivervine. Some people chalked it up to pure coincidence, but others started gossiping about it being a sign of the end of the world or something.

Then the "Crying" from "the Confessional" turned into laughter and chatter. I heard Father Kristobal's voice carrying on in some weird language with another man—like two old chums sharing a beer at a bar or something. I didn't recognize the second voice or the language the men were speaking, but there was a lot of "zh" in almost every word. It was very strange.

I called out, "Hello, Zinfandel," assuming she was the second voice.

A chill brushed across my shoulder.

"It is not I," an invisible woman muttered. "Pay closer attention, darling. I do not speak Turkish."

Then I remembered a potential third specter: Saint Nicholas.

My suspicions about the identity proved correct a few moments later as soon as I heard Father Kristobal yell, "Why not?" Then an old man with a long, white beard and a red velvet cloak stepped out of the confessional and began passing out peppermint candies to all of the children. Reporters, parishioners, and children—all wet, cold and covered in slush from playing in the snow—rushed in awe to get a closer look at the stranger.

Gossip, speculation and predictions of omens littered the air. The only thing stronger filling the ether was a strong floral scent. I realize women like to wear perfume, but do they actually need to marinate in it? It was really heavy. It was stronger than Mr. Fermanski's rose garden in full bloom.

I walked toward the confessional in hopes of talking to Father Kristobal. The closer I got, though, the stronger the scent was. I couldn't see anyone nearby, but I was ready to give whoever it was a piece of my mind about the importance of keeping body fragrance to a minimum in public. Frustrated, I decided to head back to the sanctuary to find Joaquin. I found him outside, overlooking a group of children making snow angels.

We looked at the parking lot to find a mess of cars and slush, so we decided to just hang out at the church until the snow stopped and the parking lot cleared. Around 1:30 a.m., we hopped in my car, got the heater and defroster going, and set the radio to KRVN to hear what the reporters had to say about the mass. Oh yes, it was indeed the talk of the town. I almost called in to tell them what really happened, but I decided to keep the secrets to myself ... and Joaquin. I gave him the whole scoop— my interviews with the ghosts, the Comati rituals I've been attending, who the Crying Confessional was.

"What? That's crazy!"

"Yes, I know. That's what I didn't want to tell you. But it's true, I swear."

"Well, that's one helluva Feliz Navidad."

Then he reached over and kissed my cheek.

"Te amo, Manuel."

"Tu tambien, Joaquin."

Friday, Dec. 26, 2003 8 a.m.

Bad news graced the front page of today's Rivervine Tribune:

Boy dies in snow storm mayhem

By Glenda Fern, Tribune News Editor

A Christmas blizzard in Rivervine Thursday morning leaves one boy dead and several property owners without power or water.

Between midnight and 1 a.m., the temperature reached a record low of 32 degrees. Rivervine received three inches of snow during that one-hour period. Although many residents delighted in the snowy Christmas ambiance, others experienced weather-related property damage, power outages and accidents on the roadways.

The Rivervine Police Department reported thirteen vehicle-related fatalities occurring during the one-hour snow storm. One involved Constantine Adamson, the 14-year-old son of the controversial Reverend Paul Adamson, minister of the First Church of Rivervine, who has been in the news recently due to his efforts to condemn Old Town Rivervine as haunted. Detective Gary Lee, spokesman for the RPD, said the boy and his father had been arguing earlier in the evening. While the rest of the family attended Christmas Eve religious services at the family's church, young Constantine stayed at home, boycotting the holiday activity.

Before the family arrived home, Constantine grabbed the spare set of keys to his mother's car and took the vehicle for a joy ride. The youth had no previous driving experience. He made it as far as a winding, secluded area near the Vitis River when the car hit a piece of ice, crashed against a tree, and skidded into the water. The boy hit his head on the steering wheel, which gouged his left temple area, causing profuse bleeding and loss of consciousness.

Sergeant Bob Braxton discovered the vehicle on his nightly patrol. "I knew it was bad," Braxton said. "The whole car was under water and there was blood everywhere."

Lee said evidence at the scene uncovered a smoking pipe and several ounces of marijuana in a small bag inside the vehicle. The pending autopsy report will reveal if the youth was under the influence of any illegal substances at the time of death. Results are expected by Saturday.

Meanwhile, Saint Bernadette's Catholic Church, famous for its Christmas Eve "Crying Confessional," received a visit from an unidentified person dressed as an old-fashioned Saint Nicholas. At the stroke of midnight, when the crying confessional usually weeps, the character burst through the confessional laughing and passing out peppermint candies to the children.

"I think it was Satan who was at Saint Bernadette's last night," *Reverend Adamson said in a press release. "He's the one who brought the* *snow and he's the one who killed my son. He's angry because I am building* *the Spiritual Emporium and soon his reign over Rivervine will end. He* *chose the holiest night of the Christian Calendar, and disguised himself as a* *beloved figure of Christianity, just to curry favor for his evil agenda. Then he* *struck the mortal blow to my eldest child as a sign of disrespect to me. But* *the Lord's army will prevail. He cannot stop us."*

Father Armando Echeverria, spokesman for Saint Bernadette's, *claims the church had no part in the appearance of the strange character, the* *weather phenomenon or the death of Constantine Adamson.*

Rivervine Municipal Power Company was called to take care of *several trees that had fallen on the downed lines and restore power to the* *1200 block of Loam Avenue. Plumber Dick Mooney of Ace's Plumbing* *claims his dispatch center handled twenty-nine calls from Rivervine residents* *complaining of frozen pipes.*

"This was a record-breaker, all right!" Mooney said.

Wednesday, Jan. 21, 2004 5 p.m.

This was my last day at Fermata Cellars—and my birthday to boot. We had a great time. Mrs. Rhoads baked me a cake and Xavia and Sage took me out to lunch at Fermanski's.

We stopped by the Tribune office to say goodbye to Glenda.

"I'm sorry, but she's not here," Leonard the advertising guy informed us. "She's on assignment in Iraq."

"Iraq?" we all screamed in astonishment.

"Yeah, she met some soldier and decided she wanted to follow his Army troop over there."

"Well, it will make a great story," I said. "Let's just hope she doesn't get her head cut off."

Xavia put her hand on my shoulder and whispered, "She's in good hands. She'll be home in a year."

But I won't. I will, however, leave all my files here for posterity. Maybe Glenda can use them for her book someday.

Dulces sueños, mis amigos.

Epilogue

THE PASSERBY REVISITED

As I poured over each page of that provocative, poignant material, Doina poured more of that delicious, sinful concoction into my glass.

One mystery that was never resolved, though, was the origin of the fire in 1848. I added up all the clues and realized where I could find my answer.

I put down the laptop and kissed my hostess on the cheek.

"Thank you, Doina," I sobbed. "This has been the most enlightening day of my life."

"Thank you, my friend," she replied. "You are most good person."

I ran to the northwest border of the property where the weeping willow stood. The dragon-faced knot in the bark glared at me with a silent command to bow before the mighty warrior. I genuflected in sincere respect, then stared for a moment, focusing so intently that not even an A bomb could break my concentration. I didn't really know what I was doing. I just sort of imitated Bruce Lee from one of his martial arts films—you know, the way he used to gaze into his opponent's eyes? I didn't know what to expect, so I just kept staring, hoping something would happen.

As I continued gawking at the knot in the tree, something inspired me to sit my fat ass down on the ground, close my eyes and emulate all the people I'd seen on TV who meditated with their legs crossed and palms face-up on their knees. I took a deep breath. As I exhaled, a vision came to me that was clearer than a starlit sky when you're camping out in the woods.

The hallucination was so realistic that somewhere along the line I could no longer decipher vision from realty. The weeping willow started to move. The earth trembled beneath my buttocks.

The tree's roots began to pull themselves out of the ground and turn into these things that looked like crocodile feet. The metamorphosis continued with the trunk taking the form of a giant lizard, and the bark becoming its scales. The branches morphed into bat-like wings and finally, the face that had disguised itself as a knot was hidden no more. I stared at the dragon eye to eye.

It inhaled, nearly sucking me up into its huge nostrils. Then it exhaled. That's when the fire hit me, slapping me in the face. I was surprised that it didn't burn at first. It was more shocking than anything else. The pain was an afterthought.

When it reached my eyes, I saw images of a summer's night in 1848. A young, dark-haired woman lay hidden in a wine cellar alongside the corpse of a lumberjack with blood oozing out of his neck. Insanity abandoned her mind, leaving room exclusively for a melancholia and longing for the past.

In the meantime, her inebriated father was sharing opium several acres away with an elderly German-speaking man.

"Your men make my daughter sick!" the Chinaman accused. "Their amber wine gives her sores on mouth and pussy. Sores ooze and stink with musky-sweet scent."

"Your daughter makes my men sick!" the German replied. "She cannot dance anymore. The sickness has made her muscles and nerves weak. You would be best off to shoot her like the cow that she is!"

As the two men came to blows, the lowly weeping willow lay on the bank of the river, growing tired of watching the downfall of its New World home. The beast, sworn to protect the land from all enemies foreign and domestic, awakened from its slumber and rose to its duty as vigilant soldier. With one breath, its fire cleansed the area of the sickness and greed that would have otherwise ruined the sacred landscape. Once the City of Rivervine was reduced to ash, the dragon lay back down by the bank of the river, its soul returning to Land of Nod.

The storyline moved forward into the present. I found myself as one of thousands of victims of the dragon's revenge—this time, against a town whose greatest evils were ignorance and mediocrity. I plead guilty of such charges, which is why, I'm sure, the dragon penalized me along with all the others. I never attended a city council meeting. I never thought about the area's land use. I didn't care where I bought my groceries or my clothes or even my hardware. All I cared about was my cozy home with its big-screen TV so I could watch a bunch of millionaires play ball while I inhaled a couple twelve-ouncers and a bag or two of potato chips.

I tell this to you now with my deepest regret because I am so full of remorse that I can't stand it. I never thought it would be like this. I was a good person. I didn't kill anybody. I never stole anything. I only lied when I had to protect somebody's feelings. Yet here I am—awake and dead.

Glenda, please—I have let Doina down. I wanted to tell her story but I wasn't worthy of the dragon's absolution. I am so sorry that you have returned from your escapades in Iraq to a home that no longer exists. Whether you make a MIL-yun bucks, or not, please let the world know the story of Zinfandel.

The End

ACKNOWLEDGEMENTS

To my mother, **Delia**, thank you for raising me to love the art of storytelling. Huge thanks to my husband, **Eddie**, for all your support and refusal to let me give up when I thought this wasn't worth the effort. Much love to my daughter, **Sabrina**—I hope I don't embarrass you too much. And to my **Uncle Harold**, thanks for redirecting my career so I don't die a starving poet.

Kristine Logan Photography did beautiful work on the cover for this book as well as the second book in the series, *Zinfandel's Grimoire*. She also did my author photos and the professional photos used on my website and social media. She was gracious, easygoing, generous and flexible, and most importantly, she had an eye for lighting, setting and capturing my spirit along with the soul of the books. The photos were taken at **Country Heritage Winery** in LaOtto, Indiana.

The following people and organizations have contributed to my research:

• The numerous winery and vineyard owners, managers, and winemakers of the **Amador Vintners Association**. Rivervine may be a fictional city, but it was heavily inspired by the Amador County region of the Sierra Foothill AVA (American Viticultural Area). It is my nowhere-near-humble opinion that wines from this locale are the best. I especially love its zinfandel, syrah, and barbera. Thanks so much to all my friends in the wine business for advising me as I tackled this venture.

• **Fiddletown Preservation Society.** I lived in Amador County, California for twelve years, five of which were in Fiddletown, a tiny, rural community that boasts the largest and most contiguous group of Chinese buildings from a California gold rush mining community. One of the buildings—the Chew

Kee Chinese pharmacy—already has been converted into a museum. I volunteered as a docent for the museum and also led the marketing committee for the Restoration of Chinese Structures project, which was an effort to raise money to reconstruct the exterior and weatherproof the Chinese Gambling Hall and Chinese General Store. The project was completed in 2008. My experience in Fiddletown launched my interest in the Chinese-American folklore of the Gold Rush.

• **Chaw's Indian Grinding Rock**. Also in Amador County is a state historic park that features a museum, picnic area, outcropping of marbleized limestone with 1,185 mortar holes, and a Miwok village that includes a reconstructed ceremonial roundhouse (hun'ge). The site hosts events throughout the year where they invite the public into the sacred space.

• The Rev. Adamson character was inspired by a troll who found me online in 1998 through a Yahoo group for fans of the TV show *Charmed*. He claimed to be an evangelical minister named **Rev. Taylor** who ran a website called **Jesus Hates Smut**. The site no longer exists, but when it was live, his "church" advocated for white supremacy as well as the "blatant abuse and humiliation of women, especially young girls," and warned against homosexuality and Paganism. It was so graphic and offensive that it inspired me to write this book, making him the villain.

• References to Paganism were inspired by the **Sacramento Pagan Pride Project; The Sacramento Grove of the Oak** (shout out to Papa Druid, a.k.a. **Michael Gorman** and the rest of the **Order of Bards, Ovates and Druids**), and the **Sierra Madrone Grove of Ár nDraíocht Féin: A Druid Fellowship.**

• Many of the tropes involving comparative religion were

written during my degree program at **Regis University** where I took *World Religions* and *Death and Dying* as my religious studies requirements (it's a Jesuit college).

• My paranormal research experience was based on time spent with **Haunted and Paranormal Investigations, Inc.** and the **Delta Paranormal Society** in northern California.

• Anything having to do with land-use planning was inspired by my time working for the **Amador County Planning Department.**

• Archeologist **Deborah Cook** advised me on conducting research. I used this advice when writing parts for Rev. Todd Caprasen's character.

• Thanks especially to my subscribers on Patreon. Your support feeds my keyboard! Readers who would like to be part of this esteemed group of patrons of the literary arts can join at patreon.com/rivervine.

PLEASE REVIEW AND DISCUSS

The best gift anyone could give an author is to leave an honest review on Goodreads, Amazon, or other social media/blogging platform. Constructive criticism is always appreciated. Were you able to follow along with the story? Did you understand the characters and setting? What did you like or dislike?

Also, if you are in a book club, please consider discussing *Fermata Cellars*. Potential topics to debate include:

• In the battle over land-use, whose side are you on— the urban developers, ranchers and farmers, the environmentalists, the historical preservation crowd, or another interest group?

• Do you support small, local businesses or do you prefer big-box stores and chain restaurants?

• Manuel is conflicted between his deep religious beliefs and his burgeoning sexual orientation. Do your personal spiritual beliefs accept the LGBTQ+ community?

• Have you ever been inside a haunted building? If so, did you think it (the haunting) posed a safety hazard or nuisance?

• Manuel ends up leaving the safety and security of the United States to fight for freedom and justice in Mexico. What do you think should be done to help improve life for people in third-world countries?

ABOUT THE AUTHOR

Author Gwen Alyce Clayton reads in the barrel room of Country Heritage Winery in LaOtto, Indiana. Hair and makeup by Angie Gibson. Photo by Kristine Logan Photography. Copyright 2020. Used with permission.

Gwen Alyce Clayton is an independent author, copy writer, and journalist whose work has been published in local newspapers and magazines throughout the United States. Her mission is to write quality novels and modern folklore that inspire readers to think critically while enjoying the wonder of things not yet known. She lives in Ashland, Kentucky with her husband, Eddie. Clayton holds a bachelor of science degree in public administration from Regis University. Visit her website at gwenclaytonwrites.com.